AGAINST ALL ODDS

AGAINST ALL ODDS

NATALE GHENT

Harper*Trophy*Canada™
An imprint of HarperCollins*PublishersLtd*

Against All Odds
Copyright © 2011 by Natale Ghent.
All rights reserved.

Published by Harper*Trophy*Canada™, an imprint
of HarperCollins Publishers Ltd

Harper*Trophy*Canada™ is a trademark of HarperCollins Publishers

First edition

HarperCollins books may be purchased for educational, business, or sales promo-
tional use through our Special Markets Department.

HarperCollins Publishers Ltd.
2 Bloor Street East, 20th Floor
Toronto, Ontario, Canada
M4W 1A8

www.harpercollins.ca

Library and Archives Canada Cataloguing in Publication
information is available upon request

ISBN 978-1-44340-625-3

Printed and bound in the United States
HC 9 8 7 6 5 4 3 2 1

For Darcy

CHAPTER ONE

A Mysterious Storm

In the night sky over Green Bottle Street, dark clouds gathered like demons. They swirled in strange patterns, blocking out the moon and the twinkling stars. The wind picked up, throwing litter across the yards and streets below. Flashes of yellow lightning pulsed within the clouds, illuminating the Odd Fellows as they slept innocently in their beds.

If they'd been awake, Boney, Itchy, and Squeak would have seen the ghostly silver craft appear from the storm clouds and glide with a low, otherworldly hum above their sleepy town. They would have seen the whirling coloured lights and the tractor beam searching menacingly over the rooftops.

But they were not awake. No. They'd brushed their teeth and kissed their parents good night and gone to sleep right away, like all good boys do . . .

. . . *As if.*

"What the heck was that?" Boney said into the mouth of the Tele-tube as a huge clap of thunder rattled the glass in his bedroom window.

The Tele-tube was Squeak's invention, a clear plastic tube that ran from window to window between the boys' bedrooms. Used for covert communication, the tube connected Boney's house to Squeak's and Squeak's to Itchy's, leaving Squeak in the middle to relay messages from Itchy to Boney and back again.

Boney scoured the turbulent sky, craning his neck to get a better look. "Where did all those crazy clouds come from?"

"Fascinating." Squeak's voice floated into Boney's room through the tube. "It appears to be some kind of atmospheric electrical anomaly."

"I hope it doesn't ruin your secret project plans," Boney said.

Squeak cleared his throat. "Why would it?"

"Can't you just tell me what it is?" Boney asked. "You've been working on it every night for weeks."

"I told you, you'll find out tomorrow."

Boney slouched in his chair. "Well, I hope Henry's okay with all this thunder."

"Henry is not burdened with human phobias," Squeak said. "He's a rooster. Besides, it's illogical to ignore the fact that we just reshingled the clubhouse with 245 margarine lids from your aunt's supply. It's completely leak-proof."

Boney rolled his eyes. "Thank you, Mr. Spock. Are you going to talk like a Vulcan for the rest of our lives?"

Squeak sniffed. "Would you rather I emulated a Klingon?"

"What happened to Leonardo da Vinci?" Boney asked. "You used to love him before we started watching *Star Trek*."

"So . . . you'd rather I speak Italian?"

"Just forget I said anything. Man, it's hot." Boney wiped the sweat from his brow as he peered through his window again. "Those clouds are really weird. It's like there's a tornado coming or something. The sky was perfectly clear two seconds ago." Boney suddenly jumped up from his chair. "Hey, did you see that?"

From across the gap that divided the two houses, Squeak could be seen pressing his face against his bedroom window, searching the sky through his authentic World War I aviator's goggles. "I see nothing out of the ordinary . . ."

Boney pointed furiously at the ominous clouds. "There's something out there!"

Squeak opened his mouth to reply but his voice was drowned out by a deep drum roll of thunder. He seemed frozen in place, his goggled eyes wide and searching, his small form illuminated with strobes of lightning. And then the thunder stopped as abruptly as it had started.

Boney sat down, holding the Tele-tube to his lips. "I'm sure I saw something out there. But whatever it was, it's gone. And so are those weird clouds." He stared at the sky. It was clear once again, the moon and stars appearing as if nothing out of the ordinary had happened.

"How very odd . . ." Squeak muttered.

"What does Itchy think?" Boney watched as Squeak spoke into the tube leading to Itchy's room. He could see Squeak shaking his head.

"He's being completely illogical, of course," Squeak reported. "He thinks it's the end of the world. And he's still complaining about the humidity."

Boney guffawed and was about to make a sarcastic comment when his aunt's shrill voice pierced the dark.

"Boneeey! Get to bed!"

Boney groaned, but he knew better than to argue with his aunt, even if it was summer vacation. He'd lived with his aunt and uncle since he was a baby, after his mother and father disappeared in a mysterious ballooning accident. His aunt was strict and didn't put up with wilful behaviour.

"Gotta go," Boney whispered into the tube. "See you tomorrow."

"Three o'clock—*sharp*," Squeak reminded him for the tenth time that day. "I have to help my dad rewire a house so I can't make it until then."

"What about Itchy?" Boney asked. "What's he doing tomorrow?"

"He's going grocery shopping with his mom."

"All day?"

"He sleeps until noon, remember?"

"Oh yeah, right," Boney mumbled. "My aunt doesn't believe in such laziness. She wakes me up at eight every morning, no matter what. I hate getting up early. It's so . . . boring."

"I know," Squeak said. "But at least getting up won't be such a shock for you when school starts again—which is only five weeks away, by the way."

Boney scrunched up his face. "Please, don't remind me."

"Anyway, don't forget to feed Henry before you come over," Squeak said. "He becomes irrational if he isn't fed before noon."

"How can you tell when a rooster's behaving irrationally?" Boney wondered.

Squeak stared at him through his bedroom window. "Are you making a joke?"

Boney shook his head. "Never mind. I always feed him first thing in the morning, so don't worry."

Squeak saluted. "Roger that."

Boney saluted back. "Over and out."

CHAPTER TWO

THE SECRET MACHINE

In the morning, everything was as normal as it ever was on Green Bottle Street. Mr. Johnson was already up mowing his tiny, perfectly manicured lawn. Mrs. Pulmoni's cat was streaking across the street with Itchy's terrier, Snuff, in hot pursuit. The paper boy was riding down the middle of the sidewalk, carelessly throwing newspapers into flower beds and onto front lawns.

Boney yawned and wiped the beads of sweat from his lip as he climbed the rope ladder to the clubhouse. It was only eight-thirty in the morning but already the heat was unbearable. He stuck his head through Escape Hatch #1, rubbing the sleep from his eyes. Pulling himself up, he dug into his pocket and produced a handful of cornmeal, scattering it on the clubhouse floor. "Come and get it, Henry . . . breakfast."

The rooster appeared, sauntering like an arrogant cowboy toward the cornmeal, his bright red comb flopped to one side. He was a teenager now, his white feathers painted with a splash of black on his tail. If he had been disturbed by the strange storm the night before, he didn't show it. He winked a yellow eye at Boney, waiting for his morning scratch. Boney rubbed him on the neck below his beak, the rooster squinting with pleasure.

"It's hard to believe we thought you were a hen." Boney chuckled, remembering when Squeak had brought the chick to the clubhouse all those months ago. "I'm glad you're a rooster—this is a boys-only club. Although I'm sure Aunt Mildred would have loved some fresh eggs."

Henry ruffled his feathers at the very idea, then cocked his head, listening to Boney's voice as though he understood every word. He waggled his comb and set to work picking and scratching at the cornmeal.

Boney looked fondly around the clubhouse. It was the perfect sanctuary for three Odd Fellows. There were shelves of food for Itchy, who was tall and pale with crazy red hair and a bottomless appetite. There was a bookcase stacked with reference material for Squeak, with his goggles and gap-toothed smile and his unparalleled intellect that made it impossible for him to fit in the way normal kids did. And there was the big red easy chair in one corner for Boney. He'd purchased it with his Invention Convention prize money the year before and had sat in it every day since, thinking up hare-brained schemes.

Boney reclined in his chair, one foot slung over the arm. It was going to be a long day without Squeak and Itchy to help him kill time. Reaching over, he pulled a book from the reference library and began to read. But he'd already read the book five times before so he replaced it and grabbed a deck of cards instead. Sitting at the table, he played endless games of solitaire, snapping the cards loudly as he went. When he was tired of that, he bounced a ball against the clubhouse wall until it ricocheted off the leg of his easy chair and flew down the hole of Escape Hatch #3. Then he napped in his chair until his aunt called him in for lunch, where he ate three peanut butter and jelly sandwiches and drank two glasses of milk. Returning to the clubhouse, Boney played even more games of solitaire, then languished in his chair until the hands on his watch reached three o'clock. "Finally!" he said, jumping to his feet. He gave Henry a quick scratch and streaked down the fire pole in Escape Hatch #2. Pushing through the bushes, he burst into Squeak's backyard.

Squeak was already waiting. "You're three minutes late."

Boney looked around. "Where's Itchy?"

Squeak pushed on the bridge of his goggles. "Late, as always. If he doesn't show up soon, we're going to start without him."

"Who are you starting without?" Itchy appeared around the corner of the garage, munching on a triple-decker tuna salad sandwich, his hair a tangled red tumbleweed rolling around on his head. He was wearing his usual baggy jeans, a lime-green bandana twisted and tied around his pale forehead, and the Superman T-shirt Boney had lent him the year before.

"Hey, that's my shirt," Boney said.

Itchy looked down as if seeing the shirt for the first time. "Is it?"

"You know it is! I lent it to you ages ago."

Itchy smirked. "Obviously I didn't, or I wouldn't have worn it."

"Come on. Everything you own is purple after your mom's latest dyeing binge."

"It's green, actually. Everything's lime green now." Itchy pointed to the bandana on his forehead.

Squeak peered skeptically through his goggles at the bandana. "Yeah . . . I'm not so sure that's a good colour for you . . . It makes you appear . . . pastier than usual . . ."

"It absorbs the sweat from my forehead."

Squeak winced. "Uhhh . . . yeah . . ."

"Green, purple, whatever," Boney said. "That's still my Superman shirt. You'd better not get any tuna juice on it."

"Fine. I'll just take it off right here." Itchy raised the hem of the shirt.

"Gentlemen, please," Squeak interrupted. "Can we get on with it?"

"Sure," Itchy said, popping the last of his sandwich into his mouth. "If that's okay with Officer Boneham, T-shirt Detective." He shot a wry look in Boney's direction.

Boney sighed.

Itchy turned to Squeak. "So . . . what's this 'big secret' you've been working on?"

Squeak stood next to a large, canvas-draped object, unable to hide his excitement. "This, my Odd friends, is the result of endless nights of painstaking research. It's the most incredible achievement of my life to date."

"More incredible than the Apparator?" Boney asked.

Squeak nodded. "Yes. Though the Apparator is a revolutionary ghost-detecting device."

"And it won the grand prize in our school's Invention Convention last year," Boney added.

"And it helped us get even with Larry Harry and Jones and Jones at the Haunted Mill," Itchy said. "So long, Fart King!"

The Odds burst out laughing.

Squeak adjusted his goggles. "I can assure you with all confidence, gentlemen, that the invention I'm about to unveil is much, much more incredible."

"So what is it already?" Itchy reached for a corner of the canvas cloth.

Squeak pushed his friend's hand away. "Please . . . allow me." He motioned for Boney and Itchy to step back. "Gentlemen . . . I would like to present my master-piece." He grabbed the edge of the cloth and whipped it ceremoniously to the ground.

Itchy and Boney gasped. *"An airplane?!"*

The sunlight glinted off the plane, which was streamlined and smooth and made entirely of some kind of silver-grey metal. The craft was as long as Squeak was tall—about four feet in total—and had a blue comet painted on the tail. Squeak gestured reverently toward the plane. "This, gentlemen, is no ordinary craft. This is the *StarSweeper 5000*."

Itchy scratched his tangled mop of hair. "A carpet-sweeping what?"

"*StarSweeper 5000*," Squeak corrected him. "This beautiful machine is going to win the thousand-dollar prize at the Flying Fiends Amateur Aircraft Competition."

Itchy turned to Boney. "Do you have any idea what he's talking about?"

Boney shrugged.

"It's the best amateur flying contest in the entire area," Squeak said. "People come from all over to see it. The calibre of the entries is really high. And the best part is they encourage you to be a bit crazy. That's why I used a magnetic positron eliminator in the *StarSweeper's* design."

Itchy stared blankly back at him. Squeak produced a small, worn newspaper article from his shirt pocket and flipped it open with a quick motion of his hand.

"Read it for yourselves, gentlemen, in the *Tickleview Times.*"

Itchy snatched the piece of paper from Squeak. Boney huddled next to his friend as they read the particulars of the contest, Itchy's lips moving silently over the words.

"It says the contest is tomorrow," he said aloud. "And that they encourage 'creative problem solving.'"

"Affirmative," Squeak answered. "The sky's the limit."

Itchy handed the article back to Squeak. He pulled a chocolate bar from his pants pocket and ripped open the wrapper as he walked in a slow circle, examining the plane. "You're not seriously thinking of flying this thing, are you?"

Squeak blinked behind his goggles. "Of course. Why else would I have spent all this time building it?"

"Well . . . it's kind of . . . small . . . isn't it?"

"I'm not flying *in* the plane. It's radio controlled." Squeak produced a square black metal box from his military messenger bag. The box had a silver toggle, a bunch of coloured switches and buttons, an antenna, some dials, a throttle, and a small lever. He flipped the toggle switch, causing the antenna to extend to full length.

"Cool," Boney said, examining the controls.

Itchy grunted through a mouthful of chocolate. "We came all the way over here for this? People have been flying radio-controlled planes for years."

"You live next door," Boney said.

"Yeah, but I made a special trip over thinking we were going to see something really cool."

Squeak rested one hand lovingly on the plane. "This *is* really cool. It's a totally innovative design. It has a titanium-alloy body with a variable-sweep forward horizontal stabilizer and dual-engine propulsion thrusters."

"Oh, well then," Itchy scoffed, throwing his hands in the air. "Why didn't you say so in the first place?"

Boney ran a finger along the body of the plane. "It's really beautiful, Squeak. You did an amazing job."

"Seems kind of flimsy to me." Itchy tapped the tail and tested the rudder.

Squeak brushed Itchy's hand from the plane. "It's not flimsy. Titanium is remarkably resilient — when used properly."

Itchy curled his lip, unconvinced.

"I have full confidence in the design," Squeak asserted. "I studied the schematics of hundreds of airplane models. I'm going to win that thousand-dollar prize if it kills me." His voice cracked.

"It just might," Itchy muttered, stuffing the last of his chocolate bar into his mouth.

Squeak ignored him and handed Boney a thick, meticulously detailed instruction manual for the plane.

Boney flipped through the pages. "Wow. You wrote this all by hand?"

Squeak nodded. "Winning this prize will give us a chance to enter NASA's Revolutionary Vehicles and Concepts Competition. I was hoping you could help me with the test run."

"Oh no," Itchy protested. "You can't launch that thing here. There's no room. You'll hit a tree or crash through a window in someone's house or something."

"Don't be illogical," Squeak said. "I have no intention of launching the *StarSweeper* in a populated area." He disappeared into his garage then reappeared with a large red metal flatbed wagon. "I need you to help transport the plane to the test site."

"What test site?" Itchy asked.

"Starky Hill."

"Starky Hill?!" Itchy choked. "That's thousands of

feet—straight up! It's way too humid for that type of activity." He tightened his lime-green bandana.

"It's 612 feet up, to be exact," Squeak said. "And it's the site of the flying competition. I want to get a feel for the place before the contest tomorrow. Besides, it's totally secluded. No one will be able to observe us there. I don't want any spies stealing my design before the contest."

Itchy snorted. "Spies?"

"It's been known to happen." Squeak squinted at the sky. "They're everywhere."

Boney and Itchy squinted at the sky, too. It was completely clear, and blue as a robin's egg.

"You're not worried about that storm last night, are you?" Boney asked.

Squeak stared back at him. "There are more things in heaven and earth than are dreamt of in your philosophy."

Itchy groaned. "Oh great. Now he's quoting Spock."

"That's Shakespeare," Squeak said.

"Spock, Shakespeare, who cares? What could that storm possibly have to do with spies?"

Squeak refused to answer.

Itchy clawed at his hair. "Oh sure . . . spies fly around in clouds, causing thunderstorms so they can steal people's stupid ideas."

Squeak folded his arms across his chest. "I see no reason to stand here and be insulted."

Boney rubbed his chin. "I don't think I'd recognize a spy if I saw one."

"Of course you wouldn't," Squeak agreed. "That's why they're spies." He checked his watch. "It's three-twenty. We should get going. Help me lift the *Star-Sweeper* onto the wagon. Boney, you take the tail. Itchy, the other wing — *gently*. Okay, gentlemen, on the count of three . . ."

Boney and Itchy obediently reached for the plane.

"One . . . two . . . three . . . lift."

"Hey, it's light!" Itchy exclaimed as the boys easily lifted the plane onto the wagon.

"As I already explained, it's a revolutionary design." Squeak draped the plane lovingly with the tarp. He turned to his friends. "All right. Boney, you man the tail to keep her steady while I pull the wagon. Itchy, you cover the wing."

Squeak gripped the handle of the wagon and began carefully hauling the plane through the backyard. The boys navigated the length of the garage to the sidewalk and trundled along the street. They rolled past Itchy's house, where his father could be seen practising his Elvis routine in the living room. They rattled past Mrs. Pulmoni's place, where her cat peacefully sunned itself on the porch, and past Mrs. Sheider's schnauzers barking savagely through her screen door.

At the end of the street, Squeak pulled the wagon gingerly down the curb, careful not to jostle the plane. The boys worked their way across the intersection and up the curb on the other side. As they progressed down the street, cars slowed to get a better look. Neighbours gawked from lawn chairs and from behind closed curtains.

The boys crossed the forked road leading down to the Haunted Mill. Boney shuddered as he remembered the ghost and how it had terrorized their bully, Larry Harry. But the Odds had nothing to fear now, because the ghost was gone and Larry Harry had been reduced to a crying baby. He wasn't a threat anymore. Besides, Larry had spent the first six weeks of summer at his family's cottage. The Odds hadn't seen him once since the end of school.

When they reached the base of Starky Hill the boys began to methodically climb, taking turns pulling the wagon. By the time they reached the top of the cliff, the three friends were panting like tired dogs.

"We made it," Boney gasped.

Squeak checked his watch again. "Four o'clock. It took exactly forty minutes to get here."

"I'm dying of thirst," Itchy croaked, wiping the sweat dramatically from his neck.

Squeak produced a canteen of water from his military messenger bag and handed it to his friend. Itchy removed the cap and guzzled water as if he'd just walked across the Sahara Desert.

Boney yanked the canteen from Itchy's hands. "Save some for the rest of us." He took a big swig, and then handed the canteen back to Squeak.

Itchy sniffed indignantly. "You don't have to be so rude about it." He peered over the edge of the cliff and gulped. The cliff's jagged face dropped vertically to the rocks below. "That's a long way down."

Squeak nodded. "It's the perfect place for a flying competition. It provides an adequate amount of airspace to practise the necessary manoeuvres."

Boney held up the *StarSweeper*'s manual. "Are we ready for the test flight?"

Squeak produced the black control box from his bag. Boney and Itchy uncovered the plane and lowered it like a delicate cake to the ground. Squeak flipped the toggle switch on the control box, raising the antenna. "Gentlemen . . . prepare to launch."

"Wait!" Boney shouted. "There's someone else here!"

CHAPTER THREE

SPIES

B oney pointed to where a small figure moved along the ridge of the cliff in the distance. "Someone's watching us."

Squeak quickly covered the *StarSweeper* with the canvas tarp and shielded his eyes from the sun with his hand. "I can't see anything."

Itchy pointed like a frantic baboon. "I see him! Over there."

Pulling his antique brass telescope from his messenger bag, Squeak snapped it to full length and began earnestly scanning the landscape. "I see him now. He's running away."

"Let's get him!" Boney said. "Come on!"

Itchy tightened his lips. "I'm not going anywhere."

Squeak blinked behind his goggles. "Affirmative. It would be illogical to leave the *StarSweeper* unattended."

"Fine," Boney said. "I'll go myself, then." He took off running, jumping over boulders and skittering through gravel. His arms pumped as his sneakers kicked up clouds of dust. The mysterious figure ran in front of him, sprinting toward the treeline at the base of the hill. He was dressed entirely in black and wearing a shiny, black motorcycle helmet, his face hidden behind the mirrored visor. He was small but incredibly fast, like some kind of space leprechaun, his arms and legs whirling like pinwheels as he ran. Boney ploughed down the hill, determined to catch him. Several times, the spy looked over his shoulder, the sun flashing off his visor as he quickened his pace.

"Hey!" Boney shouted. But the spy only ran faster. Boney gritted his teeth, his arms and legs a blur. "I'm going to catch you!" he yelled as the distance between him and the spy began to shrink. Encouraged, he ran harder still, getting closer and closer. But just when he thought he would catch him, the spy dashed into the dark forest and vanished.

Boney rushed into the woods, skidding to a stop in front of a big maple tree. His chest heaved as he searched the woods, his hair clinging to his sweat-soaked forehead. Sunlight filtered softly through the branches. Starlings chucked and whistled in the treetops. The spy was nowhere to be seen. He'd disappeared without a trace.

Boney looked around for several more minutes before giving up and dragging himself back up the cliff to where Squeak and Itchy waited.

"What happened?" Itchy called out as Boney approached. "Did you catch him?"

"Were you able to identify him?" Squeak asked.

Boney shook his head. "I couldn't tell who it was." He leaned his hands on his knees to catch his breath. "He was wearing a black helmet. He had the visor down so I couldn't see his face."

"Who do you think it was?" Itchy asked. "Do you think he was spying on us?"

Squeak chewed on his nails. "That's the only logical explanation for wearing a helmet in this heat."

"But how would he have known we'd be here?" Itchy wondered. "Maybe he followed us from the house."

Boney shook his head again. "I don't know. But he was little—and fast."

"Little and fast . . ." Itchy repeated, as though that description would somehow help them solve the riddle. "Could it be someone on the cross country team at school?"

Squeak paced back and forth, wringing his hands and muttering to himself. "No one could possibly have known we were going to test-run the *StarSweeper* here today . . ."

"Well, whoever he is, he's gone now," Boney said. "And I don't think he'll be back. I chased him all the way to the woods."

Itchy turned to Squeak. "Do you still want to test-run your plane? Because it's almost suppertime."

Squeak consulted his watch. "According to my timepiece, it's only four-thirty-six."

Itchy clutched his stomach. "I know. But I usually have a pre-supper snack. If I don't eat now, I'll be dead soon."

Squeak sighed, rustling in his messenger bag and producing a sandwich. "I've been carrying it around for a couple of days, but it's probably still edible. You may want to give it a sniff just in case . . ."

Itchy plucked the sandwich from Squeak's hand, unwrapped it, and stuffed it into his mouth until his cheeks bulged like a crazed chipmunk's. "Mmm . . . peanut butter and honey. I love when the honey gets all crunchy."

Boney grimaced. "Yuck."

Itchy finished the sandwich and stripped the green bandana from his forehead. He shook it out before wiping his mouth, then tied the bandana back around his head.

"Are you through?" Squeak asked.

Itchy patted his stomach. "That should hold me off for a few minutes."

"Good." Squeak did a quick scan of the horizon with his telescope. When he was satisfied the spy was no longer around he carefully uncovered the plane.

Boney opened the instruction manual, leafing through the pages until he found the ignition sequence. "Okay, let's run her through her paces. Are we ready?"

His eyes locked on Squeak's.

Squeak raised the antenna on the black control box, finger poised over the switches. "Gentlemen, record the time for the log, please."

Itchy consulted his Mickey Mouse watch. "Ten to five."

"Ten to five," Squeak repeated, then nodded at Boney.

"Ignition," Boney said.

Squeak moved to flip the switch. There was a blinding flash as a giant beam of light shot out of the sky. The boys stood frozen in their sneakers, the beam of light throbbing over them, Itchy's screams barely audible over the roaring wind.

CHAPTER FOUR

MISSING TIME

The wind howled around the Odds, throwing dust and gravel in the air. The strange light pulsed and scanned, and the boys gaped vacantly as a series of smaller coloured lights began to flicker on and off in rapid succession.

Behind a tree in the woods, the spy watched in secret, shooting dozens of photos as the huge cone of light began to slowly rotate over the three friends.

Then, just as suddenly, the lights flickered off and were gone. The wind immediately stopped. The dust settled around the boys. They looked at each other, dumbfounded, their hair horribly dishevelled.

"What are you waiting for?" Boney asked Squeak. "I said ignition."

Squeak wiped the dust from his goggles and stared back in confusion. "What happened to your hair?"

Boney ran his hand over his head. "You should talk. You look like you've seen a ghost."

The two boys turned to Itchy. His hair was even more clownlike than usual.

"What?" He looked at his watch. "Hey! It's ten after five. We'd better get this over with because I'm starving."

Squeak raised his eyebrows. "You said it was only ten *to* five."

"Did I?" Itchy took his watch off, shook it, and held it to his ear. "It's still ticking . . ."

"Something's not right," Squeak said.

Itchy licked his lips and spat. "Man, it's dusty out here. I'm going to die of thirst."

"Seriously . . . there's something really unusual going on," Squeak said.

Boney held up the airplane manual. "Is anybody at all interested in the test run?"

"Uh, yes, of course, in a minute . . ." Squeak dug his telescope from his bag and raised it to his eye to scan the surroundings one more time, then abruptly lowered it, cleaning the lens with the corner of his T-shirt. "I can't see a thing."

Itchy looked over his shoulder. "Does anyone else feel strange?"

"Strange how?" Squeak asked.

"Stranger than usual. I feel like I have a big hole in my stomach."

Squeak frowned. "But you always have a hole in your stomach."

"Can we get on with it?" Boney said. He blew the dust off the manual and looked for the proper page. "Are we ready?

Squeak nodded.

"Ignition."

Squeak engaged the switch on the black control box and the *StarSweeper* roared to life. The jet engines whined, creating small tornadoes of swirling dust behind the plane.

"Lights," Boney called out over the noise of the engines.

Squeak flicked another switch and a set of small lights appeared along the length of the plane, with several red lights on the tail and one large white light at the front.

"Flaps."

Squeak moved a lever back and forth. The flaps on the wings responded with small waving movements.

"Prepare for takeoff."

The plane lurched forward, engines whining loudly as it slowly rolled toward the edge of the cliff. Squeak taxied the plane to within ten feet of the edge, then turned to Boney. Boney drew in his breath.

"Takeoff!"

Squeak pushed the throttle. The engines began to sing, and the *StarSweeper* skipped along the ground, wheels bouncing over the gravel as the plane picked up speed. It streaked toward the edge of the cliff, dropped over the side, and was gone in a puff of dust. Boney and Itchy gasped. Seconds later, the plane reappeared, rising in the air, and tearing across the sky like a supersonic dragonfly.

"You did it!" Boney and Itchy cheered, jumping up and down.

Squeak smiled as he worked the controls, the plane arcing in a wide circle around the sun.

"Do a loop-de-loop!" Itchy said.

Squeak's fingers moved easily over the buttons. The plane shot into the air, engines surging louder as it climbed, then slowly curved back, scribing a perfect loop as it lassoed the clouds. Squeak pushed the plane harder, the craft twisting like a corkscrew until he let it drop in a spiral free fall.

Itchy clutched his hair. "It's going to crash!"

The plane suddenly powered back to life and zipped across the sky. Itchy applauded. Squeak smiled. He flew the plane around, testing its maximum velocity and control for several minutes before bringing it in for a landing. Its wings dipped up and down as it navigated toward the cliff. Hitting the parched ground, the plane jounced across the gravel, its engines winding down until it came to a stop in front of the boys.

"Amazing!" Boney shouted.

Squeak beamed. "Gentlemen, our test flight was a success."

"You're definitely going to win the grand prize," Boney said, clapping him on the back.

"Yeah, that was great," Itchy agreed. "But can we go home and have supper now? We're going to be late."

While the boys were congratulating themselves and packing up their things, the spy spirited away through the trees.

Back on Green Bottle Street, the three friends manoeuvred the plane into Squeak's garage, stowing it carefully. Squeak pushed on the bridge of his goggles.

"Don't forget the competition starts at nine a.m., so we'll have to leave at seven-thirty at the latest," he said. "That gives us forty minutes to get to Starky Hill and enough time to set up."

Itchy complained under his breath about the early start time. Boney saluted, then cut through the hedge at the back of Squeak's house to his aunt and uncle's yard.

He was hoping his aunt hadn't noticed he was late for dinner.

But he had no such luck. She was standing in the kitchen, red gingham tea towel over one arm, wringing her hands. His uncle sat at the kitchen table, looking cagey.

"William Boneham!" his aunt barked the second Boney stepped through the door. "Where have you been?"

Boney opened his mouth to answer but his aunt cut him off sharply.

"Supper should have started by now! Do you think I'm running a restaurant? And what have you been up to? You're a filthy mess. Just look at your hair!"

Boney ran his hand through his hair, glancing warily at the stove to where a big silver pot stood waiting on the burner. He didn't mind missing dinner, especially when his aunt made one of her awful soup-can recipes. He tried to appear casual. "Oh, that's okay, Auntie, I'm really not that hungry."

"Nonsense!" she snapped.

"Now, Mildred," Boney's uncle sputtered through his moustache. "Boys will be boys."

"Oh phooey," his aunt said. "Anyone with any common sense would appreciate a nice, warm meal and actually show up on time for dinner. Your friend Itchy understands."

Boney stared at her in confusion. "What do you mean?"

His aunt straightened the gingham tea towel on her arm. "He's been here at least three times in the last half hour, leering through the kitchen window like some kind of cotton-headed vampire. I gave him at least half a dozen oatmeal cookies but he just keeps coming back for more. The boy must have a tapeworm, he eats so much." She paused, tilting her head. "But he wouldn't take any of my casserole . . ."

Boney opened his mouth to speak but his aunt cut him off again.

"Then Mrs. Sheider called, complaining that Itchy was gaping through her windows as well. But she didn't have her glasses on at first and she thought he was a prowler so she let the dogs out to chase him off. What on earth has gotten into that boy? Doesn't Itchy's mother cook?"

Boney glanced at his uncle for confirmation but his uncle simply looked the other way, leaving him on his own to deal with his aunt. "Uhhh . . . that's not possible," Boney said. "Itchy was with me and Squeak all afternoon. We weren't bothering anyone. We were up at Starky Hill."

His aunt scowled. "Don't argue with me, young man. It's rude."

"But Auntie . . ."

His aunt silenced him with a wave of her wooden spoon. "Not another word. Go wash, then take a seat and eat."

Boney knew better than to protest further. He washed in the bathroom, then returned and pulled a chair from the table, sitting obediently while his aunt busied herself reheating his dinner. She huffed and puffed, clattering dishes and pots in a show of irritation. When at last she placed Boney's plate in front of him, she stood sentry, waiting for his reaction.

Boney stared at the steaming pile of grey glop on his plate. He didn't dare ask what it was. All he knew was that it must be horrible if even Itchy didn't want any. Looking mournfully at his uncle, he tentatively lifted his fork, his hand shaking as he stared at the mound of goo. With a quick breath, Boney stabbed his fork into the glop and raised a heaping portion to his mouth. He stuffed the food in, chewed twice, and swallowed. His eyes widened. "Hey! It's actually good!"

His aunt beamed. "Of course it's good. I used a recipe from the cookbook you gave me for my birthday." She grabbed a yellow cookbook from the shelf beside the stove and held it up, reading the title out loud like some overly pleased housewife on a TV commercial. "*One Hundred Delicious Dummyproof Dishes*. Isn't that a fun title?"

Boney looked at his uncle and grinned. His uncle winked back.

"But it's not as good as the title I dreamed up for my own book," his aunt said, placing the yellow cookbook back on the shelf. "*Seven Thousand Sensational Soup-Can Suppers.*"

"More like *Dozens of Dinner Disasters*," Boney muttered into his casserole, but, thankfully, his aunt didn't hear him. She was too busy looking dreamily off in the distance, no doubt fantasizing about book signings and international fame.

"I have fifty-two recipes so far," she mused. "I have a lot of cooking to do!" She flicked the red gingham tea towel from her arm and cracked it at some phantom bug that only she could see.

Boney shuddered at the thought of her soup-can cookbook. He dug his fork into the tasty glop on his plate, shovelling it in. It seemed he was starving after all.

His uncle relaxed in his chair as Boney scraped his fork across his empty plate. His aunt loaded his plate again, knocking the sides of the pot joyfully with her wooden serving spoon.

"It's amazing there's anything left in the house at all, what with Itchy coming around every five minutes." She placed the empty pot in the sink and began to scrub it.

Boney just smiled dutifully as he inhaled his second serving. When he was finished, he ate three oatmeal cookies for dessert and excused himself, bringing his dishes to the sink. "Thank you, Auntie, that was delicious." He gave his aunt a small peck on the cheek.

His aunt smiled brightly. Boney saw an opportunity to approach her about the flying competition. He patted his stomach with exaggerated satisfaction.

"I'm sure glad to have eaten such a nutritious meal tonight. It will help me get through the day tomorrow."

The smile left his aunt's face. "What's going on tomorrow?"

"Oh," Boney answered as casually as possible, "Squeak's entering his model airplane in a race over at Starky Hill."

His aunt pursed her lips.

"He's been working on it for weeks," Boney continued. "And we get to help him transport the plane to the competition. We have to leave really early, so I won't be at the table for breakfast." He gave his most endearing smile, hoping his aunt would overlook the part about missing breakfast.

She harrumphed, whisked the tea towel from her arm, folded it neatly, and hung it on the handle of the oven. "I'll make sandwiches then. And I suppose Squeak and Itchy will be needing lunch, too. It's not like their parents will be so organized. Though I'd need a dump truck full of sandwiches to satisfy that red-headed friend of yours."

"Yes, ma'am," Boney agreed, to avoid further scrutiny. He quickly made his exit and trotted upstairs.

In his bedroom, Boney yawned. He was thinking of going over to Squeak's house but the very idea made him feel exhausted. "Must have eaten too much casserole," he murmured, lying down on his bed. He was just closing his eyes when he heard a rustling sound from beneath the towel that hid the Tele-tube. Squeak's small voice floated into the room.

"Boney . . . are you there? Over."

Groaning from bed, Boney flopped into the chair in front of his window. He removed the towel and held the end of the tube to his lips.

"Boney here."

He waited for Squeak to speak, but there was silence on the other end of the line. Boney's head bobbed sleepily. He gave another big yawn. "Are you there, Squeak?"

"I'm here," Squeak answered.

"What's on your mind?"

More silence. Boney's eyes drooped as he waited.

"I can't stop thinking about our experience today," Squeak finally said.

"What experience?"

"At Starky Hill. I think something happened."

"Of course something happened. We tested the *Star-Sweeper 5000* and she passed with flying colours."

Squeak cleared his throat. "Yes, she did . . . but I'm talking about something else . . . something strange."

"Okay . . . what, exactly?"

There was another pause. "Missing time."

Boney looked at his alarm clock. "Missing time? What do you mean?"

"When I asked Itchy what time it was, he said it was ten to five. But when I looked at my watch before the test flight, it was ten after five. Somehow, we lost twenty minutes."

Boney pulled on his chin. "Maybe Itchy made a mistake."

"No. I checked my watch as well."

"So . . . what do you think happened?"

"I don't know. Itchy said he felt strange . . ."

Boney snorted. "Yeah, well, Itchy *is* strange, in case you hadn't noticed. My aunt said he was staring through our kitchen window like a vampire."

"What? That must have been unnerving."

"To say the least. And then my aunt said that he kept coming over begging for cookies but he wouldn't eat her casserole."

"When?" Squeak asked.

"Today."

"But he was with us all day . . ."

"I know. It doesn't make any sense."

"There's definitely something weird going on."

"Yeah," Boney agreed. "But do you want to know what's really weird? My aunt's casserole was actually good."

"Really?"

Boney rubbed his stomach. "I ate two plates. But I'm so tired now. I can barely keep my eyes open."

"Me too," Squeak said. "I don't know why I'm so exhausted."

Boney yawned loudly. "Do you really think all of this strangeness has to do with missing time?"

Squeak stalled. "Well . . . I have some theories . . ."

"Let's hear them."

Squeak sniffed into the tube. "I can't say right now. I need more evidence before I draw a conclusion."

"Just give me a hint. Maybe I can help you figure it out." Boney waited for Squeak to answer but grew impatient. "Just tell me."

Silence.

Boney rolled his eyes. "What does Itchy think?"

"He's not answering the tube."

"Well, I can't help you if you won't tell me your theories."

"I don't want to make a big deal of things until I have some hard evidence," Squeak said. "I prefer the concrete, the graspable, the provable."

"Is that a Spock quote?"

"*Star Trek*, season one, episode twenty-one. 'The Return of the Archons.'"

"Ah yes, of course." Boney chuckled. He stretched sleepily. "Well . . . if you're not going to let me in on your ideas, I'm going to bed. I'm so tired, I feel like I ran a marathon."

"You did do a lot of running today," Squeak said. "But what's my excuse?"

Boney shrugged. "Maybe it's the heat."

"Yes . . . possibly . . ."

"Anyway, I can't keep my eyes open anymore. I'll see you in the morning for the competition tomorrow, okay?"

"Okay."

"Good night, Squeak."

"Good night, Boney."

Boney tossed the towel over the end of the Teletube. Rising wearily from his chair, he changed into his pyjamas and climbed heavily into bed. Pulling the sheet over his shoulders, he gave another long yawn. "I feel so strange," he murmured before falling into a very deep sleep.

CHAPTER FIVE

THE FLYING FIENDS AMATEUR AIRCRAFT COMPETITION

Boney woke at seven in the morning feeling rested after nearly twelve hours of sleep. Determined to be early for Squeak's big day, he rushed to get ready. Racing down the stairs and into the kitchen, he slowed long enough to peck his aunt on the cheek and grab the large paper bag full of sandwiches she'd made for the competition. Then he flew out the door and shimmied up the clubhouse ladder to feed Henry. Tossing a handful of cornmeal on the floor for the rooster, Boney shot down the fire pole and ran through the bushes into Squeak's backyard. But despite his efforts to arrive early, Squeak beat him again. He was already waiting expectantly in front of his garage, wearing his favourite *Star Trek* T-shirt—the one with the image of Spock's face airbrushed in front of the starship *Enterprise*. As usual, Itchy was nowhere to be seen.

Boney skidded up to the garage. "Are you ready to win the big prize?"

Squeak saluted. "Affirmative."

"What is the big prize again?"

"A thousand dollars cash, a year's membership to the Flying Fiends Amateur Aircraft Club, and paid entry to the NASA Revolutionary Vehicles and Concepts Competition."

Boney nodded. "Not bad. Did you figure out what happened yesterday during the test flight?"

"No," Squeak said. "But I think it's connected to the electrical storm we experienced the other night."

"I wish you'd tell me your theory."

Squeak pushed on the bridge of his goggles but said nothing. Boney held up the bag of sandwiches.

"My aunt made lunch for us."

"That was nice of her."

"And I have some money for drinks." Boney pulled a handful of change from his pants pocket.

"Good thinking," Itchy said, shuffling up to his friends. He was eating a muffin and carrying a basket with three black-and-grey-striped kittens rolled together like socks. He was wearing the green bandana again, but this time, instead of the Superman T-shirt, he wore a with a picture of several forlorn-looking

nt and a giant powder-blue phone num-

ss the back. Between the pink shirt and

a, his tangled red hair looked as though

u get the kittens?" Boney asked. "And

hirt?"

d. "My mom . . . she joined some club

cats."

into the basket. "Fascinating."

uess. It's better than knitting terrible

verything in the house weird colours

ow we've got kittens running all over

sneezed and wiped his nose on the

shirt. "She wanted me to wear this

he competition. I've got shirts for you

led two more pink T-shirts from his

led them out.

smile. "Gee . . . thanks . . ." He looked

Squeak didn't respond but simply took the T-shirt and pulled it over his *Star Trek* shirt. Boney resigned himself with a shrug and did the same. He turned to look at Squeak. Squeak blinked back at him. The kitten shirts were so long they looked like pink minidresses.

"Perfect," Boney muttered.

"What's in the paper bag?" Itchy asked, gesturing with the basket of kittens.

Boney hid the bag behind his back. "Nothing."

"Smells like egg salad sandwiches." Itchy reached for the bag.

Boney dodged him, holding the bag at arm's length. "They're for later."

"But I'm hungry now."

"I just saw you eat a muffin," Boney said.

"That was breakfast."

"So?"

"I'm still hungry."

Boney scoffed, handing the bag of sandwiches to his friend. "You can have ONE."

Itchy placed the basket of kittens on the ground and ripped open the bag. "There must be a dozen in here." He pulled a sandwich out and took a big bite. "Mmm . . . delicious egg salad . . . but I still prefer peanut butter and jelly . . ."

Boney folded his arms. "I'll keep that in mind for future reference. Try not to eat the kittens while you're at it."

"We'd better get going," Squeak said, studying his watch. "I want to be sure to get the best position on the cliff for the race."

The boys wheeled the cloaked *StarSweeper* from Squeak's garage, careful not to bang the wings against the door frame as they manoeuvred the craft outside. The wheels of the wagon squeaked like a small flock of dim-witted birds, the edge of the tarp brushing the tops of the tires. The Odds hauled the plane down the walk and out to the street, making their way toward Starky Hill. Squeak pulled the wagon while Boney steadied the plane from the back by the rudder. Itchy followed, carrying the kittens and eating egg salad sandwiches until Boney shouted at him to save some for later. While they were walking, several cars slowed down on the street to gawk at the three friends. One driver even yelled something unintelligible out his car window.

"Did you understand what he said?" Itchy asked.

"It sounded like 'I'm calling the police,'" Boney said.

Squeak paused. "Who was he talking to?"

Boney shrugged. "Who knows?"

By the time the boys reached the bottom of Starky Hill, the sun was winking behind the border of trees to one side of the cliff.

Boney wiped the sweat from his brow. "It's going to be another hot day." He looked up the hill toward the cliff. The hill seemed even higher in the morning light.

"Maybe we should have a rest before we drag the plane up this mountain," Itchy said, opening the bag of sandwiches.

Boney scowled. "How many sandwiches have you had?"

"I need the energy to keep me going."

Boney wrenched the bag from Itchy's hands. "I told you to save some for later."

"Fine. You don't have to be such a jerk about it," Itchy pouted.

"Do you have to eat everything in sight?" Boney said. "My aunt told me about the cookies."

Itchy made a face. "What cookies? I wouldn't touch anything your aunt baked."

"Take that back."

"Make me."

Squeak stepped between them. "Gentlemen, please. I can't hear myself think with all this bickering."

"Sorry," Boney apologized. He turned with irritation toward Itchy. "I hope you brought some water for those kittens."

Itchy produced a water bottle and a small dish from his knapsack. "Is this good enough for you?"

"Yeah, sure. As long as you don't drink it all yourself." Boney reached for the handle of the wagon.

Squeak intercepted him. "If you don't mind, I'll pull the *StarSweeper*."

Itchy gave Boney a self-satisfied look. Boney sneered back but kept his comments to himself.

Squeak huffed and puffed, pulling the wagon up the hill. He had to stop several times to catch his breath, refusing Boney and Itchy's offers of assistance. At the top of the hill, the boys could see a group of people setting up tables and colourful banners and signs. To one side of the tables, a makeshift wooden stage had been built. Clusters of eager spectators were already gathered on blankets with picnic baskets, waiting for the contest to begin. They turned to look at the Odds, particularly Itchy. Some pointed and whispered as the boys walked by.

"Do you know these people?" Boney asked Squeak.

"I've never seen them before."

"Then why are they all staring at us?"

"Perhaps they're just curious about the contestants." Squeak stopped to dab the sweat from his face.

"They seem to be interested in Itchy." Boney nodded to a blanket full of children who were staring openly.

"Maybe it's his hair," Squeak said.

Boney smirked. "Can you blame them? They probably think he's a clown who escaped from the circus. Anyway, it looks like we're the first contestants here."

"Not quite," Squeak said. "Someone's beat us to it." He gestured toward a dark figure near the edge of the cliff. It was the spy from the day before!

"What's he doing here?" Boney growled.

"Maybe he never left," Itchy said.

Squeak glared through his goggles. "He took the spot I wanted." He handed the wagon over to Itchy and marched up to the registration table, casting furtive glances at the mysterious contestant.

A balding man with a face like a half-baked apple pie sat behind the registration table, mopping the sweat from his brow. He smiled pleasantly as he took Squeak's name, then scratched it off the list and gave him a registration number. "Nice shirt," he said.

"*Star Trek*'s my favourite show," Squeak answered.

The man gave him a quizzical look. "I didn't know there were kittens on *Star Trek*."

"Huh?" Squeak looked down, his face turning red when he saw the pink kitten T-shirt. He'd forgotten he was wearing it. "Uh, yes, thank you. It's a charity dedicated to saving homeless cats."

The man nodded. "It's nice to see young people involved in good causes."

"Yes, thank you," Squeak mumbled. He turned and shoved the registration number at Boney, who helped pin it to the back of Squeak's shirt. When Boney was finished, Squeak took the handle of the wagon from Itchy and wheeled the *StarSweeper* along the cliff, scouting for the next-best position, muttering bitterly under his breath the entire time. He glowered at the spy. "This would have been easier if someone hadn't stolen my spot."

When at last they settled on a location, the three boys positioned the wagon, Squeak fussing over the precise placement of his rig.

"Should we remove the tarp from the plane?" Boney asked.

Squeak looked at the spy's well-hidden entry. "No."

Boney licked his finger and held it in the air. "There's a bit of a headwind. That could slow us down."

"The *StarSweeper* will cut right through it." Squeak continued to fiddle with the plane as more and more contestants arrived.

"Oh no," Itchy suddenly said, pointing to the bottom of the hill. "Who invited those guys?"

It was Simon Biddle and Edward Wormer, the Odds' schoolmates and lifelong scientific adversaries . . . and Larry Harry and Jones and Jones!

CHAPTER SIX

CRASH AND BURN

"Hey, doofus!" Larry Harry called out as he parked his entry beside Squeak's. "You may as well go home because you know I'm going to win."

Itchy leapt in front of Larry, shoving his skinny white fist into the bully's face. "Oh yeah? Says who?"

Larry shrank away in terror, hiding behind his hands. "Just kidding, just kidding!"

"You'd better be kidding," Itchy snarled, waving his fist at Jones and Jones, who cowered behind Larry. "Now move your wagon! We don't want you anywhere near us."

"Okay, okay." Larry ducked his head and ordered Jones and Jones to move his wagon to the other side of the field.

But just as Larry Harry wheeled his rig away, Edward Wormer pulled up beside Squeak, parking his wagon next to the *StarSweeper*. Simon Biddle parked on the other side and began immediately adjusting the tarp covering his craft so that no part of his secret entry would be prematurely exposed.

"Fancy meeting you here," Wormer greeted the Odds, his metal braces flashing in the sun. "Ooo, nice shirts," he mocked. "What are you? The kitten club?"

Itchy sheltered the basket of kittens with his hands.

Squeak scowled. "These shirts are for a good cause. And by the way, I'd rather you didn't set up next to me."

"What difference does it make?" Wormer quipped. "I'm going to win, regardless of where I park my wagon."

Boney clenched his jaw. "I could suggest another place to park your wagon."

Biddle snickered into his hand.

"That goes for you, too, Biddle," Itchy jumped in.

Wormer nodded toward the spy, who seemed to be watching and taking notes from his position at the other end of the cliff, his identity hidden behind the mirrored visor of his black helmet. "Who's the ninja?" he sneered at Squeak. "A friend of yours?"

Boney crossed his arms. "We thought it was your mother, worm breath."

Squeak turned to Boney with a confused look. "Why would we think it's his mother? That's a totally illogical response."

"Ha, nice try." Wormer glared at Boney.

Boney grimaced back. "You're going to eat our dust, Wormer." He turned to Squeak and whispered from the corner of his mouth. "Do you think we have anything to worry about?"

Squeak pushed on the bridge of his goggles. "Of course not." But he looked over his shoulder at the spy all the same. "What could he possibly be writing?"

"I'm thirsty," Itchy said, pulling the water bottle out of his knapsack.

"Don't drink the kittens' water!" Boney barked.

Itchy bristled. "I told you I wouldn't do that. What kind of person do you think I am?"

"I can answer that." Wormer produced a newspaper from his bag and tossed it at Itchy's feet. "Read it and weep, paleface."

There, on the front page, blazed a huge head-line: MYSTERY CLOWN BOY TERRORIZES TOWN! Beneath the headline was a blurry photo showing little more than a streak of pasty skin and red hair.

Itchy placed the kittens on the ground and snatched the paper up. "What's this got to do with me?"

Biddle scoffed. "Recognize the face?"

Itchy studied the photo.

"Oh, come on," Wormer goaded. "You know it's you."

Itchy looked at him like he was crazy. "Me? Are you kidding? This could be anyone, it's so fuzzy! It could be a sasquatch, for all I know."

"A red-headed sasquatch," Biddle said.

Boney took the paper from Itchy. He and Squeak pored over the photo and skimmed the article, then looked at Itchy with concern.

"What?" Itchy said. "You don't actually think it's me, do you?"

Boney paused. "It says you've been peering into people's windows."

"And stealing food," Squeak added. "Someone's blueberry pie was taken right off their windowsill . . ."

"I would never do that!" Itchy insisted.

Boney held up the paper and read aloud: "Multiple sightings throughout the town . . . voracious appetite . . . stolen food . . ."

Itchy tore the paper from Boney's hands. "It's not me! I swear! Look at the picture. Does that look anything like me?"

Boney and Squeak stared blankly back at him.

Itchy clawed at his hair. "I'm telling you, it's not me!"

Biddle snorted. "Oh sure. There are hundreds of pasty, red-headed clown boys running around town, stealing food, and looking through people's windows."

Wormer's braces flashed. "Admit it. You just can't control yourself." He made an eating motion with his mouth.

Squeak and Boney had to restrain Itchy as he lunged at Wormer, his skinny white legs kicking wildly in the air. "It's not me!" he shouted, throwing the newspaper at Biddle's feet.

"Fine, already," Biddle said. "It's some other pasty, red-headed kid. What do I care?"

"You'd better care!" Itchy threatened, kicking dust at Biddle like an angry chicken.

Squeak loosened his grip on Itchy's arm. "I'm sure it's just a mistake."

"Here," Boney said, digging into his pocket and slapping some quarters into Itchy's hand. "Go get some lemonade — and bring some back for me and Squeak."

Itchy took the quarters, grimaced at Biddle and Wormer, then punted the newspaper as he made his way over to the refreshment booth. Moments later, he was back, empty-handed and wearing Boney's Superman shirt. The kittens jumped from their basket and hid in the grass, hissing and growling when they saw him. Boney frowned.

"What are you doing?" he asked. "And where's your kitten shirt? I suppose it's okay for us to walk around looking stupid but not you?"

Itchy looked at him stoically.

"What happened to the lemonade?" Boney demanded. "I told you to bring some back for me and Squeak. What is wrong with you?"

Itchy just stared at him, then turned and silently walked away. The kittens hissed and growled as he left.

"Geez," Boney cursed, shaking his head.

Squeak pointed to the newspaper, a concerned look on his face. "Do you think it really is Itchy . . . ?"

Boney snatched the paper from the ground and slammed it into a trash can. "I don't know. I don't want to hear another word about it."

A minute later, Itchy returned, carrying three cups of lemonade. He was wearing the pink shirt again.

Boney took a cup of lemonade. "That's more like it."

"I came as fast as I could," Itchy said. "There's a big line for drinks." He took the opportunity to scowl at Biddle and Wormer as he handed a cup to Squeak.

Biddle and Wormer scowled back. Squeak just downed the drink in a single shot and began fussing with the tarp on his plane again. While he did this, more onlookers and contestants arrived, until there was a line of more than twenty entries fringing the edge of the cliff. Some of the people gawked at Itchy, pointing and whispering behind their hands the way the others had done earlier.

"Maybe if you took that green bandana off, you wouldn't attract so much attention," Boney said.

Itchy sulked. "But it keeps the sweat from dripping into my eyes."

Boney gave him a look.

"Fine." Itchy tore the bandana from his forehead and crammed it in his back pocket. "Satisfied?"

Boney shrugged.

At nine o'clock sharp, the loudspeaker crackled and a tall man in a straw fedora began to speak, his voice engulfed in a blare of feedback. Wormer and Biddle shouted in pain, covering their ears with their hands until the feedback subsided.

"Weenies," Itchy jeered, unwrapping a chocolate bar and taking a huge bite. "As if I'd go around stealing pies . . ."

Boney eyed him with suspicion. "Where'd you get that chocolate bar?"

"I bought it at the concession stand. Why?"

Boney stared at his friend.

"What? Do you think I stole it?"

Boney raised his hands in truce. "I'm not accusing you of anything. Where are the kittens?"

Itchy spun around, searching the grass. The kittens were playing with some children across the field. He grabbed the basket and ran to retrieve them, but returned with the basket empty. "The family wants to keep them."

"All three?"

Itchy nodded. He was about to launch into an explanation but was interrupted by another blare from the loudspeaker.

"Ladies and gentlemen . . . we are thrilled to welcome you to the twenty-third annual Flying Fiends Amateur Aircraft Competition. Before we begin, let me regale you with a bit of history . . ."

The announcer droned on as the sun rose higher in the sky. Cicadas buzzed in the trees, children ran around, onlookers picnicked, and contestants shifted anxiously in their sneakers. All except for the spy. He stood with pen and notebook at the ready, scribbling intently. Squeak bristled.

"Maybe he's writing his will. He's going to need it after today."

"Or a grocery list," Boney said, trying to lighten the mood.

Itchy brightened. "I could use some groceries."

Boney shook his head. "You're not making a good case for yourself."

"I can't help it if I get hungry all the time," Itchy said, clutching his stomach.

The announcer finally drawled to a close. He ended his speech with a request for donations as he removed his hat and wiped his brow with the red kerchief he would later use to signal the start of the race. "You all know the rules," he bellowed. "Be creative! First craft to circle the orange halfway pole and return across the finish line takes the prize. May the best man win! Gentlemen . . . please . . . take your marks."

There was a sudden flurry of activity as the entrants uncovered and manoeuvred their planes to the proper spots on the cliff edge, each desperately trying to catch a last-minute glimpse of the other entries. Wormer's plane looked like some kind of modified World War II Mustang. Biddle's was a strange sphere made from concentric wooden rings that revolved around each other, and had to be launched from a giant golf tee. Larry Harry's craft was a balsa wood biplane. The other entries included a miniature microlight plane; a model Twin Otter plane; a helicopter; some kind of crazy, wingless rocket ship that looked like it was made from old margarine tubs; a Fokker F28; a Brewster Buffalo; and an assortment of scratch-built prop planes.

Itchy pointed scornfully at Biddle's wooden sphere. "What is that?"

Biddle's nose twitched. "Only the most revolutionary craft known to man, pie boy."

"Ha!" Itchy laughed, turning to gauge Squeak's reaction.

But Squeak was too busy staring through his telescope, hoping to get a closer look at the spy's entry. "It looks like some kind of stainless steel body," he said. "Single tail thruster with dual jet engines. There's no way his plane will be faster than the *StarSweeper*. It looks far too heavy to outclass us."

Boney pulled on his chin. "Forget about it for now, Squeak. The race is going to start any second."

Squeak closed his telescope and stuffed it back into his bag. He held the black metal control box with both hands, a thin bead of sweat forming on his upper lip.

"Contestants," the announcer called. "Start your engines!"

Dust filled the air as the planes jumped to life, some backfiring, some whining, some sputtering slowly then spinning to a high-pitched buzz. Larry Harry's balsa wood plane exploded instantly in a cloud of black smoke, its propeller flying off and landing in the gravel behind the announcer. Itchy and Boney laughed and pointed until Larry Harry and Jones and Jones stomped off in a rage, dragging the remains of their entry away on their wagon.

Squeak tested the rudder and flaps on the *Star-Sweeper*, spooling up the engines in preparation for takeoff. Wormer revved his engine in challenge. Biddle increased the velocity of his wooden sphere, the concentric circles whirling faster and faster around each other until the entire craft was just a blur. Squeak inched the throttle forward, until the *StarSweeper*'s jets began to scream. The three boys glowered at each other, fingers poised for battle.

The announcer raised his red kerchief against the yellow glare of the sun. He held it there for what seemed like an eternity, and then dropped his arm like a guillotine.

"*Go!*"

Squeak released the brakes. The *StarSweeper* streaked off in a shower of gravel, Wormer's Mustang buzzing just inches behind. The margarine-tub rocket arced in the air and sizzled over the edge of the cliff, crashing and melting like processed cheese on the rocks below. Biddle's sphere rolled off its tee, whipped around in the dirt, then zipped over the edge and shattered, landing in a heap of kindling next to the melted rocket at the bottom of the cliff. The Fokker F28 and Brewster Buffalo droned behind the Mustang, hot on the *StarSweeper*'s tail. Squeak pressed the little yellow button and the *StarSweeper* blasted forward, leaving the other planes behind like insects in the clouds.

Itchy and Boney cheered, their fists pumping "Go, Squeak, go!"

"Ha ha!" Itchy gloated. "The prize money is ours!"

Squeak looked over his shoulder with glee and noticed that the spy's plane hadn't even left the ground.

The spy nodded his helmet in Squeak's direction as he held his control box to one side and pushed the ignition button. There was a flash of blue light and a strange, low whir, like the sound of a powerful turbine spinning into action. The ground began to tremble and all heads turned to see blue flames shooting from the back of the spy's plane. The spy pressed another button and the jet ripped off the cliff with an earth-shattering boom, the shock wave knocking several bystanders to the ground with its force. The crowd gasped in unison. The spy worked the controls, sending the jet straight into the sky in a big loop before zipping past Squeak's plane, only to slow down and cruise easily behind the *StarSweeper*. The crowd roared.

Squeak gritted his teeth as he pressed the red button on his control box. The *StarSweeper* surged forward, its wings vibrating against the force of the air current. He turned to look at the spy, who was looking back at him, the sun glinting off his visor. The spy raised his finger and wagged it at Squeak before pressing another switch. The afterburners blazed, and his plane roared to within inches of the *StarSweeper*.

"Go faster!" Itchy yelled.

Squeak hit the throttle. But no matter how fast the *StarSweeper* went, it could not shake the spy's plane. Squeak tried dodging and looping and outmanoeuvring, but the spy was stuck to him like glue. He glanced over his shoulder again and was sure he could hear laughter as the spy stood, finger hovering over the controls of his plane. There was a moment's pause, then the spy pressed a button. A small hatch retracted at the top of his jet and a mechanical arm appeared from the opening, a mini-gun attached to the end.

"Noooooo!" Squeak howled as the gun hammered, tearing the *StarSweeper* into a thousand pieces that rained down from the sky in a shower of flames. Squeak gaped in disbelief, the control box slipping from his hands onto the gravel as the spy's jet looped around the halfway pole and returned to the cliff, lapping the other planes and landing with awe-inspiring precision.

"We have a winner!" the announcer shouted.

Boney's jaw dropped. "Who *is* this guy?!"

The spy raised his fists in victory. The crowd cheered and clapped. Squeak hid his face in his hands.

"It can't be legal to blow someone's plane out of the sky," Itchy protested.

"Well, it was certainly creative," Boney said. "I guess that makes it fair."

Squeak shook his head, muttering vacantly to himself. "Annihilation . . . total, complete, absolute annihilation . . ."

Edward Wormer poked Squeak on the arm, his own plane resting safely on the ground once again. "Looks like it's back to the drawing board for you."

"What are you talking about, Wormer?" Itchy jumped to Squeak's defence. "You didn't win either!"

Wormer's braces flashed. "Yeah, but at least my plane didn't get blown out of the sky in front of everybody. How embarrassing."

"Almost as embarrassing as getting caught stealing someone's pie," Biddle added, his head thrown back in laughter as he walked away.

"Not as embarrassing as that stupid wooden sphere at the bottom of the cliff!" Itchy yelled after them.

But Biddle and Wormer just laughed all the louder.

The loudspeaker crackled as the announcer took the stage. "Ladies and gentlemen . . . please join me in the winner's circle to present the award. What a show of fiendish creativity by the winning competitor!"

"Come on, guys," Itchy grumbled. "We don't need to stand here and watch this."

Squeak sighed in defeat. "No . . . it's okay. I'd like to meet the person who kicked our butts. Maybe I'll learn something." He shuffled toward the stage, shoulders hunched, Boney and Itchy trailing behind him.

The crowd thundered as the announcer placed a gold medal around the spy's neck. Another man handed the spy a big gold trophy and the giant-sized winner's cheque for one thousand dollars.

"Ladies and gentlemen," the announcer drawled. "Please put your hands together for Sam Moss, the winner of this year's Flying Fiends Amateur Aircraft Competition!"

The crowd exploded.

Itchy made a face. "Sam Moss? What kind of name is that? I bet he's all weird and warty and covered in green fuzz."

"That's probably why he hides behind that visor," Boney grumbled. "To cover his fuzzy green face."

Just as Boney said this, the spy removed his helmet. The entire crowd gasped, but none louder than the Odds.

"*It's a girl!*"

Chapter Seven

Things Get Odder

"I told you he was weird!" Itchy said.

Boney and Squeak stared, thunderstruck, at the girl on the stage. She shook her shining brown mane of hair and flashed a brilliant smile.

Edward Wormer pointed at the Odds. "Ha ha! How does it feel to be obliterated by a girl?"

"Shut up, Wormer!" Itchy snapped. "She beat you, too."

"Boo hoo," Simon Biddle taunted. "Maybe you can get your kittens to fly your plane next time."

The announcer's voice boomed over the sound system. "Tell us, Sam, what's your winning secret?"

The girl took the microphone and flashed another perfect smile. "My own special brand of organic, sustainable rocket fuel!" She squealed and jumped up and down with excitement.

The crowd cheered.

"Thank you so much," the girl gushed, her hazel eyes sparkling. "My name is Samantha Moss and it was a pleasure to beat you today." She held her trophy in the air as the cameras popped.

Boney and Squeak continued to gape at the stage.

Itchy scratched at his hair. "She owes us a new plane. And she can afford it now, too, seeing as she won the one-thousand-dollar prize." He turned to his friends for support, but they just kept staring at the girl. Itchy elbowed Boney. "Hey, did you hear what I said?"

Boney fluttered out of his trance. "Oh yeah, right."

Itchy nudged Squeak. "What do you think, Squeak? Should we ask Miss Mossy Teeth to pay for the damages?"

"Uhhh . . . damages . . . yeah . . ." Squeak's voice trailed off.

Itchy snapped his fingers in front of Squeak's face. "Earth to Squeak, come in, Squeak."

Squeak stood in a daze. "Oh . . . what? Sorry . . ."

"Come on," Itchy said, putting his arm around his friend. "There's no sense standing here feeling sorry for ourselves. Besides, I'm hungry."

Boney handed Itchy the bag of egg salad sandwiches. "Just finish them. I've lost my appetite."

Itchy opened the bag and happily extracted a sandwich. "The day wasn't a total loss," he said, trying to console his friends. "At least the kittens got adopted."

He munched on the last of the sandwiches as Squeak and Boney took turns pulling the wagon home, lost in their own thoughts. Once again drivers slowed down to gawk at the boys and speed away.

"What's gotten into everybody?" Itchy asked.

"Maybe they saw your picture in the paper," Boney said.

"It's not my picture," Itchy garbled through egg salad. "How many times do I have to tell you that?"

"Sure, of course."

Itchy gestured with a half-eaten sandwich. "Maybe they saw Squeak crash and burn at the flying competition . . ."

Boney stopped in his tracks. "Now that's just mean."

"It's fine, it's fine," Squeak intervened. "I wouldn't blame anyone for gaping at us after that dismal performance today. Let's just try not to kill each other, okay?"

Itchy shrugged. "Sure, I don't care."

Boney gave him a look and continued to pull the wagon.

When they approached Green Bottle Street, the boys couldn't help but notice a big moving van parked on the corner at 24 Walker Avenue.

"Looks like someone's moving in," Boney said.

Squeak pushed on the bridge of his goggles. "I didn't even know that house was for sale."

Itchy craned his neck to get a better look. "It's been empty for years. I wonder who bought it?"

A red station wagon pulled up behind the truck and Samantha Moss jumped out, Flying Fiends trophy in hand. She waved cheerfully at the Odds.

"Oh no . . ." Itchy groaned. "It's her!"

A tall skinny man in a lab coat stepped out from the driver's seat, wearing a pair of goggles as thick as Squeak's, his short white hair sticking out in every direction. He looked distractedly at the boys, pulled a box filled with pipettes and beakers from the back of the car, then scuttled into the house, and slammed the door.

Squeak blinked. "Who the heck was that?"

"Who cares?" Itchy said. "Let's get out of here before old Mossy Teeth tries to talk to us." He grabbed the wagon by the handle and began to run, the wagon clattering down the sidewalk, drawing the neighbours to their windows with the commotion. In his rush, Itchy nearly flattened Mrs. Pulmoni's cat, sending it screeching into the street, which cued Mrs. Sheider's schnauzers to start savagely barking. Then Snuff joined the fray, chasing the cat across the road and up Mr. Peterson's tree just as he was gliding into his driveway on his bike. Ringing his bell like a fire alarm, Mr. Peterson swerved to avoid the cat, crashed his cruiser over the curb, and landed in a cursing heap at the side of the road.

"Hey, wait up!" Boney called, ignoring Mr. Peterson's misfortune.

"Of all the neighbourhoods, she had to pick ours," Itchy complained.

Squeak trotted behind him, stealing a glimpse as Mr. Peterson righted himself and limped his bike toward his garage. "Maybe she's just visiting."

"Not with our luck," Itchy muttered.

"Well, at least she's not moving onto our street, right?" Boney said.

Itchy waved the empty sandwich bag. "She's right on the corner. It doesn't get much worse than that."

"Do you think she'll go to our school this fall?" Squeak asked.

"Don't say school!" Itchy freaked. "It's still summer vacation. I don't want to think about school!" He picked up the pace, smashing the wagon up Boney's drive and over the lawn to the giant oak tree that supported the Odds' clubhouse. Dropping the handle, he shimmied like a monkey, carrying the empty kitten basket up the rope ladder and into the clubhouse.

Boney and Squeak stared at each other at the base of the tree.

"What an odd day," Squeak said.

"Very," Boney agreed.

Itchy's red mop popped out of Escape Hatch #1. "Hey! Are you guys coming up or what?"

Boney and Squeak climbed the ladder. Itchy was already at the table, stacking peanut butter and honey crackers in a neat pile. Henry was scratching at some cornmeal that Itchy had scattered on the floor. Itchy rubbed his hands greedily together. He grabbed a cracker stack and was just about to deposit it in his mouth when a girl's voice called out from below.

"Hello!"

The Odds froze, staring at each other in terror.

Itchy gagged. "It's her!"

"Hello!" the voice called again. And then there was the distinct sound of someone clambering up the ladder.

"Hide!" Itchy hissed.

"Where exactly?" Boney asked. But then he zipped to his easy chair, throwing one leg over the arm, all casual-like.

Itchy gobbled his stack of crackers, pushing them furtively into his mouth, crumbs flying everywhere. Squeak stood, feet glued to the floor. They waited, holding their breath until a girl's head appeared through the escape hatch. It was Samantha Moss.

"Hi!" she said, giving another cheerful wave. She pointed at Henry. "Oh—a rooster! He's a leghorn, right?"

Boney and Squeak exchanged surprised looks.

"Actually, yes," Squeak answered.

"Don't talk to her," Itchy barked, cracker crumbs spraying from his mouth. He turned to Samantha. "You can't come in here. This is a boys-only club. No girls allowed! Get it? Even our mascot's a boy." He gestured wildly at Henry.

Squeak cleared his throat. "We believed he was a hen when I first introduced him . . ."

"Who cares?" Itchy snarled. "He's a boy now. Any-one with two eyes in their head can see that!"

"Oh . . . I'm sorry," Samantha apologized. "I didn't realize. I was interested in adopting a kitten, but I see that I'm . . . interrupting something. I'll just . . . leave then."

"Good!" Itchy shouted, as Samantha lowered her head and began climbing back down the ladder. He wiped his hands together, swallowing the last of his crackers with a big gulp.

Squeak stared at his friend in bewilderment. "Uh . . . that was kind of rude . . . don't you think?"

"Rude?" Itchy bobbled his red mop. "Have you gone soft in the head? If we start letting girls into our club, there's no telling what will happen."

"Like what?" Boney asked.

Itchy flapped his hands around. "I don't know. Bad things!"

"You could have been nicer about it," Squeak said.

"Nicer?!" Itchy's jaw dropped. "She kicked our butts in the flying competition just moments ago, in case you don't remember."

Squeak stared back at him.

"She *spied* on us! She tried to steal your invention!"

Squeak raised an eyebrow. "We can't say that for certain."

Itchy turned to Boney in disbelief. "Are you hearing this? Help me out here."

"She was interested in adopting a kitten," Boney said. "You should have thought about that before kicking her out."

Itchy tore at his bramble-bush hair. "Am I the only one who isn't crazy around here? Let me spell it out for you: she's a G-I-R-L — *GIRL!*"

Boney and Squeak didn't answer.

"Fine!" Itchy growled, grabbing the box of crackers and the jars of peanut butter and honey. "Suit yourselves! But don't come crying to me when things go all weird!"

He marched to Escape Hatch #2 and attempted to grab the fire pole, fumbling the cracker box and dropping the jar of peanut butter down the hole. He snarled with frustration and eventually threw the crackers down the hole, then scowled and slid down the pole, hitting the ground with a yelp, the box of crackers exploding in a shower of crumbs.

Boney and Squeak peered down the escape hatch as Itchy grappled with the food and hobbled off. In a second he was back, climbing the rope ladder like an angry red-headed ape. "I forgot the kitten basket."

Squeak handed the basket to Itchy.

Itchy snatched the basket, wrapped his skinny legs around the fire pole, sniffed with disdain, and slid out of sight.

"What's he so angry about?" Squeak said. "I'm the one who got my invention destroyed."

Boney shrugged. "Who knows? Maybe he's upset about the newspaper article." He took the opportunity to remove the pink kitten T-shirt and place it on a hook by the reference library. "Do you want to hang out after supper?"

Squeak removed his pink shirt as well and placed it on the hook. "I don't know if I can. My dad has some kind of surprise for me."

"Oh, okay. What do you think it is?"

"I have no idea."

Boney picked up the deck of cards from the table. "Want to play a few hands?"

"Sure."

The boys sat in the clubhouse, playing cards for the rest of the afternoon, Squeak keeping score with his pencil and notebook. He peered at Boney with his best poker face. "Got any kings?"

Boney tossed his cards to Squeak. "You win. Again." He rubbed his stomach. "I'm getting kind of hungry. What time is it?"

"It's almost supper." Squeak pushed a button on his watch. The face lit up and small black-on-white analogue numbers flipped in succession, counting down to zero. "Your aunt should be calling you in three . . . two . . . one . . ."

"Boneeey!" his aunt hollered from the kitchen window. "Supper!"

Boney saluted. "Gotta go."

Chapter Eight

FROZEN MEATBALLS

Boney poked his head into his aunt's kitchen, afraid of what he might smell there. But his heart lifted when he saw the yellow cookbook open on the counter and whiffed the delicious aroma of refried beans on the stove. "Smells great!" he called out, kicking off his sneakers. "What's for supper?"

"It's a surprise," his aunt said.

Boney gulped. "Oh." Whenever his aunt cooked up a surprise it was almost always a miserable disaster. He shuffled over to the stove and attempted to open the oven, but his aunt brushed his hand away.

"Go wash your face and hands and run a comb through your hair, young man, you look like you lost a fight with a thousand dust bunnies."

"Yes, ma'am." Boney disappeared obediently into the washroom to tidy up. When he reappeared, he presented himself to his aunt for inspection. She examined his neck and behind his ears, then his fingernails, and even looked between his fingers before deeming him fit for dinner. Boney walked to the table and was just about to yank out a chair when his aunt yipped.

"Don't scrape the legs across the floor!"

Boney gently glided the chair from the table and sat politely down. His uncle was already seated, reading the newspaper. He flapped it importantly, folding it several times before smacking it down with disgust on the seat of the chair beside him. There, on the front page, was the blurry picture of Itchy. Somehow, his uncle had missed it altogether, no doubt in his hurry to read the business section. Boney moved his hand toward the paper and attempted to sneak away the page.

"Widgets are down 3.2 per cent," his uncle blustered, causing Boney to retract his hand in alarm. "How's a man supposed to make a living anymore?"

"Please, Robert," his aunt scolded. "You're going to give yourself indigestion. Now close your eyes, you two . . ."

Boney and his uncle peeked at each other in fear. At least when they knew what was coming they could prepare themselves for the shock. His uncle closed his eyes. Boney used the opportunity to sneak the newspaper page with Itchy's photo and push it into his pocket before his aunt turned around from the stove. He shut his eyes while his uncle sputtered incoherently through his moustache.

There was a flurry of pots clattering and the sound of the oven door opening and closing as plates were prepared. Boney could hear his aunt's high heels clacking sharply back and forth across the linoleum, and then the kitchen fell suddenly quiet.

"Okay, open them!"

Boney and his uncle fluttered their eyes open. His aunt stood before them, wearing a sombrero and holding two plates of steaming burritos, the red pompoms on her hat bobbling merrily back and forth. "*Olé!*" she shouted.

"Wow . . ." Boney said. He looked at his uncle, who stared at his wife, unsure how to respond.

Still grinning, she placed the dishes on the table. Boney raised his fork and jabbed at the burrito, as though expecting it to jump off his plate.

"Is this melted cheese?" he asked.

His aunt patted the top of his head. "Only the best for my boys. Now dig in while it's still hot."

Boney and his uncle did what they were told, smiling with unexpected delight when they tasted the delicious beans. They dug in with gusto, knives and forks flashing until their plates were scraped clean. When they were finished, they sat back in their chairs, rubbing their bulging stomachs, their eyes glazed with satisfaction.

His uncle stifled a loud burp. "Mildred, you've outdone yourself."

Boney's aunt smiled as she clapped the yellow cookbook shut and placed it back in its position on the shelf next to the stove. Boney leaned toward his uncle and whispered, "We'll have to get her another cookbook for her next birthday."

Boney's uncle winked. "I've got it all arranged." He tapped on his belly.

Boney winked back. He asked to be excused, then brought his dishes to the sink before going upstairs to his bedroom. Once there, he took the newspaper page from his pocket, ripped it into confetti, and deposited it in the trash. Then he removed the towel that covered the Tele-tube and placed the tube to his lips. "Are you there, Squeak? Over."

There was a rustle on the other end of the tube. "Squeak here."

Boney opened his mouth to speak, but a giant burp erupted instead.

"Ahhh!" Squeak hollered. "Why do you do that to me? We need to find another mode of communication."

"Sorry," Boney apologized. "I guess I ate too much."

"Another dinner disaster?"

Boney patted his stomach. "Actually, dinner was delicious. We had burritos with real melted cheese." He burped again, but this time turned his head politely away from the mouth of the Tele-tube.

"Lucky," Squeak said. "I'm thinking of giving my dad cooking lessons for his birthday, but I don't want to insult him."

"Yeah, that could be touchy. What was the surprise he had for you?"

"Bread. He made bread today as a surprise to celebrate the flying competition. At least, it was supposed to be bread. It turned out more like a giant white brick. He broke the breadknife trying to cut it. Then he resorted to the circular saw."

Boney shuddered. "Oh boy."

"Yeah. But then crumbs got stuck in the saw blade and the motor sparked and burned out. I told him it was somehow appropriate, given my plane's performance at the competition."

"Your plane was awesome," Boney consoled him. "Hey, I think we have some leftovers in the fridge if you want."

"No . . . it's okay," Squeak said. "I made a box of macaroni and cheese. It's not so bad if you add frozen meatballs."

"Speaking of meatballs, have you heard from Itchy?"

Squeak sighed. "His bedroom curtains are shut. I keep trying to reach him on the tube but he won't pick up. I guess he's still mad."

"About what? Samantha Moss? Or his picture in the paper?"

"We can't prove it's him."

"No . . . we can't," Boney agreed. "But do you think it's him?"

"I don't know. It kind of looks like him. And he has been acting rather strange lately."

"And he does love food."

"Yeah," Squeak said. "But I'd rather not think about it. I don't like the idea of my friend being a potential criminal."

Boney pulled on his chin. "Me neither. Oh well, maybe this will all blow over by the morning."

"Yeah."

"Do you have to help your dad tomorrow?" Boney asked.

"No. But I've agreed to spend some 'quality time' with him tonight."

"Oh." Boney couldn't hide the disappointment in his voice. "Okay then. I'll see you in the morning, I guess. Let me know if you get in touch with Itchy. I'm a bit worried about him."

"Me too," Squeak said. "Over and out."

Boney tossed the towel over the Tele-tube. What was he going to do for the rest of the evening with Itchy angry and Squeak spending quality time with his dad? He grabbed the rubber ball off his floor and began bouncing it loudly against his bedroom wall, over and over, until his aunt appeared in the doorway.

"What are you doing, young man?"

Boney threw the ball toward the wall. "I'm bored."

His aunt caught the ball mid-flight. "Then get out of that chair and come help me polish silver."

Boney's face dropped. "Whaaat?"

"Now."

Boney dragged himself downstairs to where a mountain of silver cutlery and containers waited on the kitchen table. He groaned, slumped into a chair, and began to polish. "I'll never say I'm bored again . . ."

CHAPTER NINE

DOPPELGANGERS

The next morning, Boney woke to find Itchy walking across his backyard, wearing his Superman T-shirt. Boney checked his watch: seven-twenty-five. Flipping the towel off the Tele-tube, he immediately called for Squeak.

"Are you there, Squeak? Over."

There was a moment's silence and then Squeak's voice came over the tube.

"Squeak here."

Boney launched in. "You won't believe this. Itchy's walking through my backyard wearing my Superman T-shirt. I spent hours polishing silver last night. I'm not in the mood for this. What's with him?"

"Why were you polishing silver?" Squeak asked.

Boney grunted. "Never mind. Why's Itchy up so early?"

Squeak looked out his window into Boney's back-yard. "I don't know. He doesn't even breathe before noon if he doesn't have to. What's he doing?"

"He's standing at the foot of the oak tree, staring up at the clubhouse."

"Why?"

"I don't know," Boney said. "Maybe he forgot something after his temper tantrum."

"Do you think he's still mad at us?"

Boney pulled on his chin. "Who can say?"

Itchy scuttled like a crab up the rope ladder. Boney looked over to where Squeak stood in his bedroom window. The two friends shrugged at each other.

All at once, Itchy raced back down the ladder, Henry flapping and squawking after him. Itchy jumped the rest of the way down, landing easily on his feet. He looked up at Boney and then sprinted like an Olympic athlete along the house toward the street.

"What was that all about?" Squeak said.

Boney gaped out his window. "I have no clue. But I should just give him that stupid Superman shirt if he loves it so much."

"And what's Henry so upset about?" Squeak asked.

"Maybe Itchy tried to eat his food." Boney leaned closer to his bedroom window, studying the clubhouse.

A darkly clothed figure appeared, climbing down the ladder. "Who the heck is that?"

"This is highly unusual," Squeak said. "I may be mistaken, but that appears to be Samantha Moss . . ."

"What's she doing in our clubhouse?"

"I don't know, but isn't that Itchy in my backyard?"

Boney scrunched up his face. "How'd he get over there?"

Squeak shot Boney a look across the divide between their two houses. "It's physically impossible for him to be back there. We just saw him run toward the street at the front of the house . . ."

"Unless he ran around the block in less than two seconds . . ." Boney said.

"Which is physically impossible."

Boney frowned. "This is totally weird. Come on, Squeak, we're going to get to the bottom of this."

Boney tossed the towel over the end of the Tele-tube, threw on some clothes, and raced from his room, pounding down the stairs in his sock feet.

"William Boneham!" his aunt snapped. "You go right back up those stairs and come down again in a more civilized manner. This isn't the monkey house at the zoo!"

Boney marched up the stairs, did a pirouette at the top, then minced back down the steps, making sure not to thump on the landing at the bottom.

"That's better," his aunt said.

She watched as Boney walked through the living room to the kitchen to put on his shoes. To save time, he stuffed his feet into his sneakers without untying them, crushing the backs with his heels.

"Where do you think you're going?" his aunt said.

Boney smiled as nicely as he could. "Out."

She pointed at his sneakers. "You're going to trip and hurt yourself if you don't put those shoes on properly, young man."

Boney exhaled loudly but he didn't argue. He quickly untied his shoes and put them on properly, then jumped out the kitchen door before his aunt could disapprove of anything else.

"What about breakfast?" she called after him.

"No thanks!" Boney called back. "And I won't be home for lunch either!" The screen door smacked behind him.

Squeak was waiting beneath the clubhouse.

"Samantha's gone," he said.

Boney threw his hands in the air in exasperation. "I barely made it out of the house — my aunt was being so nosy. Did you see which way Samantha went?"

"I'm not sure. I don't even know if it really was her. But did you see this morning's paper?" Squeak held up the newspaper.

On the front page was another blurry photo of Itchy, only this time he was running from a doughnut shop with a bag of day-olds in his hand.

Boney ran his hand through his hair. "This is not good." And then his eyes grew wide. "Oh no, my uncle!" Boney bolted to the front of his house and grabbed the newspaper off the lawn. Tearing the picture of Itchy from the paper, he stuffed it into his pocket so his uncle wouldn't see it, then replaced the newspaper where he'd found it. "What are we going to do?" he asked Squeak when he returned to the clubhouse.

Squeak pushed on the bridge of his goggles. "We have to find him and make him—"

But before Squeak could finish his sentence, a small figure crashed through the bushes into Boney's backyard and then back out again, running vigorously along the train tracks behind the houses on Green Bottle Street.

Squeak blinked. "I believe that was Samantha Moss."

"Come on!" Boney said. "Let's find out what's going on."

Just as he said this, Larry Harry and Jones and Jones crashed into Boney's backyard, yelling at the top of their lungs. Itchy ran behind them like a mad dog.

"Get him off meeeee!" Larry howled. He turned and threw a Snickers bar at Itchy before smashing through the bushes and running along the tracks.

The chocolate bar bounced off Itchy's chest and landed at his feet. With a lightning-quick motion, he scooped up the bar and dashed along the garage to the front of the house. Larry Harry and Jones and Jones didn't look back but kept shouting in terror as they ran down the tracks into the distance.

Boney and Squeak stared in disbelief.

"Has everyone gone completely insane?" Boney said. He turned to Squeak. "Could you slap me, please, because I think I'm having a bad dream and I can't seem to wake up."

Squeak gave him a quick slap.

"Ow!" Boney howled. "I didn't mean for you to really slap me."

"Sorry."

Boney rubbed his cheek. "We have to talk to Itchy. He's out of control."

"What about Samantha Moss?" Squeak asked.

"She can wait."

The two boys walked toward Itchy's house. They were just crossing the driveway to the front porch when Itchy's father, Mr. Schutz, leapt from the house in his white sequined Elvis costume and jumped into his old blue station wagon.

"Hi, Mr. Schutz," the boys called after him. "Is Itchy home?"

But Mr. Schutz didn't even slow down. "Sorry, boys. No time. Got an early date for breakfast with some seniors at the mall." He revved the engine and put the station wagon in gear. "Elvis has left the building!" he yelled, then tore from the driveway into the street, nearly hitting a police cruiser coming down the road.

The cruiser stopped in front of Itchy's house and two police officers climbed out. Boney and Squeak turned to leave, but the officers hollered for them to stop.

"Have you boys seen this kid?" one of the officers asked, holding up a grainy security-camera photo of Itchy stealing chocolate bars from a variety store.

Boney looked at the photo. "Uhhh . . . no, sir . . ."

Squeak gave him a sharp nudge in the ribs. Then Mrs. Pulmoni stuck her head out her front door like an angry gopher and bawled at the top of her lungs, "You kids tell that red-headed friend of yours to stay out of my yard!"

The police officers glared at Boney and Squeak. Boney shrugged, smiling sheepishly, and was just about to make up an excuse when Itchy appeared at the end of the street.

"There he is!" the officers shouted. They scrambled into their cruiser and streaked off, lights flashing, siren wailing.

Itchy dashed around the corner. And then Samantha Moss entered the scene running after him.

"They're heading toward the train tracks," Boney said. "Let's go."

The boys ran toward the tracks, cutting through the bushes in Itchy's backyard. After several hundred feet, they skidded to a stop on the gravel, chests heaving. But Samantha was nowhere in sight.

Squeak wheezed, trying to catch his breath. "She's incredibly fast."

Boney panted. "You can say that again." He shielded his eyes from the sun, scouring the length of tracks, then pointed to a small figure running in the distance. "Over there!"

The boys ran between the rails, Squeak stumbling over rocks and twigs as they went. He gestured at his goggles. "My depth perception isn't very good."

Boney suddenly stopped. He grabbed Squeak by the shirt and pulled him off the tracks, crouching down behind a bush. Samantha stood at the edge of the rails, staring at a path that forked off into the trees.

"Is that new?" Squeak whispered.

Boney shook his head. "I've never seen it before. And I know every inch of this railway line from Van Ave. to Tulsa Street."

The boys watched as Samantha reached into a small bag slung over her shoulder. She produced a strange instrument that looked like a compact silver wand. Holding the instrument in front of her, she pushed a button. Two thin metallic arms with tiny glass orbs on the ends appeared from the device. They began slowly rotating at the end of the wand like the propeller of a small plane, creating a funny purple light as they spun.

"Fascinating," Squeak said.

"What is it?" Boney asked.

Samantha held the device at arm's length, moving it in a careful arc through the air. The machine made a small ticking sound, like a Geiger counter, the ticks becoming more frequent as Samantha held it toward the mouth of the path. The ticking grew louder and more urgent, the arms spinning faster and faster until the device began to crackle like raw electricity. After several minutes, Samantha depressed the button and the metallic arms began to slow, the ticking fading as the arms folded neatly back into the device. She stuffed the wand into her bag, stepped off the railway onto the path, and slipped into the shadowy woods.

Squeak turned to Boney, his eyes the size of dessert plates. "I've never seen anything like it before. It appeared to be some kind of tracking device."

"Yeah . . . but what is she tracking?" Boney stood, peered over the bush, signalled for Squeak to wait, and trotted over to the mouth of the path. When he was sure the coast was clear, he motioned for Squeak to follow. Squeak hustled over. Boney pointed to the path. "It's new. That's why we've never seen it before. Look at the broken branches on the bushes."

Squeak studied the branches. "These breaks can't be more than a day or two old."

"But look at the ground," Boney said. "It's trampled flat."

Squeak crouched down, peering at the ground. "It appears to be thousands of sneaker prints — and all the same size and pattern. Who could have done this?"

"I don't know, but we're going to find out." Boney made a motion to leave. Squeak stopped him with a hand on his shirt sleeve and a worried look in his eyes.

"Do you think it's safe?" he asked. "I mean, it seems illogical to go searching for something we may regret finding."

Boney clenched his jaw. "What choice do we have? Itchy may be in trouble. We have to help him . . . no matter how odd he's been acting lately."

"But we're not prepared," Squeak said.

Boney sighed. "How can we prepare for something when we don't even know what it is? Consider this a scouting mission. We'll look around a bit and see what we come up with. We won't take any unnecessary chances. I promise."

Squeak raised an eyebrow. "Whenever you start making promises everything goes wrong."

"That's not true."

"Yes, it is."

"All right, maybe some of the time," Boney conceded. "But this is different. Itchy needs our help. What kind of friends would we be if we just abandoned him?"

Squeak pondered this for a moment, then nodded. "Okay."

Boney patted him on the back and began creeping along the path. Squeak followed behind so closely he was practically stepping on Boney's heels. A twig snapped and Boney abruptly stopped, causing Squeak to slam into him.

"Stop following so closely," Boney hissed.

"I'm sorry," Squeak apologized. "It's a little unnerving in here."

Boney rolled his eyes. "It's just the woods. Mr. Spock wouldn't be afraid."

"Mr. Spock carries a phaser."

Boney grabbed Squeak's arm. "Shhh! Do you hear that?"

Squeak cranked his head around, scanning the trees. "Hear what?"

The two boys listened, hearts pounding.

"I guess it's nothing," Boney said, after several nerve-racking seconds. "Let's keep going."

Squeak exhaled. Boney hunched low, Squeak mirroring his movements. He looked over Boney's shoulder. "What could Itchy possibly be doing out here? He's terrified of being in the woods alone."

"He's terrified of everything." Boney stopped dead in his tracks. "Shhh! Listen!"

Squeak stumbled into him again and scowled, adjusting the goggles on his face. "You're starting to bug me."

Boney pointed to his ears and his eyes like a commando. Squeak crouched behind an old tree stump.

"I don't hear anything," he said.

Boney put a finger to his lips. "Listen . . . It's some kind of weird hum. It comes in waves."

Squeak cupped his ears. And then his eyes widened. "Yes, I hear it. It has the same cadence as a positronic generator." He produced a pencil and notebook from his messenger bag and began scribbling eagerly.

The boys listened for a moment longer, the strange hum throbbing softly around them. Boney pointed through the bushes to where a diffuse blue light seemed to be hovering over the ground. "I think it's coming from over there."

Squeak finished his calculation, then stuffed his

notebook and pencil into his bag. The two boys inched toward the light, the humming growing louder.

Boney took cover behind a tall bush, easing the branches to one side. "Holy smokes!" he gasped.

CHAPTER TEN

A TERRIFYING DISCOVERY

Boney and Squeak peered through the bushes at a long, low grey building tucked into the trees. A strange blue light glowed from a single row of small, triangular windows running the length of the structure.

Squeak grabbed his telescope from his bag and began scouring for clues. "It looks like some kind of warehouse."

"I guarantee this wasn't here before," Boney said. "How did it get here? And what's it used for?"

Squeak continued to study the building. "It's definitely not made of concrete — that much I can tell."

Boney glanced from side to side. "There doesn't seem to be anyone around. I think we should take a closer look."

Squeak lowered his telescope. "Do you honestly think that's a good idea?"

"We've come all this way. We have to find out what's going on."

Squeak collapsed his telescope. "Fine. But if things seem even the slightest bit odd or illogical, we're getting out of here."

Boney gave him a thumbs-up. Squeak clucked his tongue, placing his telescope back in his messenger bag. They were just about to stand when a set of small, firm hands clamped them on the shoulders, pushing them back down. The boys shouted in terror.

"What are you doing here?" an angry voice demanded.

Boney and Squeak spun around to find Samantha Moss staring back at them, hands on her hips, head held disdainfully to one side. "You're going to ruin everything with your noise."

Boney jumped to his feet. "You! How did you get behind us?"

"Keep your voice down," Samantha ordered.

Boney's jaw dropped. "What are you doing running around out here?"

Samantha flicked her hair over her shoulder. "I should ask you the same thing."

"We were following you."

Samantha narrowed her hazel eyes. "Looks like you found me."

"Correction," Squeak piped up. "You found us."

"It wasn't difficult with all the commotion you're making."

Boney winced with embarrassment. "We wanted to know what you were doing in our clubhouse."

Samantha's tone changed immediately. "Oh . . . I was . . . uh . . . just checking on something . . ."

"What exactly?" Boney asked.

"Well . . . it's kind of hard to explain . . ."

Boney folded his arms and looked at the girl. "Try me."

"It's okay, it doesn't matter," Squeak said, jumping to Samantha's rescue.

"Yes, it does," Boney insisted.

"No, it doesn't," Squeak countered. He leaned toward Boney. "You're being so rude." He smiled politely at Samantha. "I was really impressed with your performance at the flying competition."

Samantha smiled brightly back. "Thank you."

"I'd love to know the composition of your jet fuel formula—if you don't mind sharing," Squeak continued, as though they were exchanging cookie recipes.

Samantha tossed her hair. "Of course. I can write it out for you, if you like."

"That would be great." Squeak dug in his messenger bag for his notebook and pencil.

Boney barged between them in frustration. "All right, already! We've had enough show and tell for one day." He turned to Samantha. "Can you at least tell us what's going on here?"

Samantha stuck her nose in the air. "That's what I was trying to ascertain until you two showed up."

"It's like nothing I've seen before," Squeak launched in. "The building isn't made of concrete. It looks like some kind of superior polycarbon-fibre composite — but I've never heard of it being used in this application." He held up his notebook. "I've been taking notes."

Samantha retrieved an identical notebook from her knapsack. "Me too."

They blushed and turned away from each other, flipping through the pages of their notebooks. Samantha pointed to an equation carefully penned at the bottom of a page. "I have to agree with your assumption. It's definitely a type of polycarbon-fibre composite. But it's never been used in this manner . . . at least, not on this planet . . . yet. Though I have read about a similar type of thermo plastic being developed for space travel. But it's just a rumour at this point. Which would lead one to assume . . ." Her voice trailed off.

"Extraterrestrial life forms." Squeak pointed to a similar equation in his notebook. "Was it the humming that gave it away?"

"Yes. And the blue light," Samantha said. "They both have frequencies similar to positronic generation but far too advanced for this world."

Squeak adjusted his goggles. "I've read of such frequencies."

Samantha pushed the hair behind her ears. "Me too. They're used to facilitate—"

"—mind control," Squeak said.

The two scientists locked eyes.

Boney threw his hands in the air. "This is all very interesting, but we're wasting valuable time here!"

Squeak ignored his friend, his eyes still trained on Samantha's. "See what I have to deal with?"

"He's right," Samantha said, breaking the spell. "We are wasting time. We should take a closer look at that building. I'd like to take a sample." She slipped her notebook in her bag and began slinking toward the building.

Boney made a face at Squeak. "See what I have to deal with?" he repeated mockingly. "Some friend you are."

Squeak shrugged, guilty.

"Come on," Samantha whispered over her shoulder.

The boys fell in line, copying Samantha's movements until the three investigators were positioned behind some weeds at a safe distance from the building.

The humming was loud there, throbbing in low waves. Samantha pulled sponge earplugs from her bag and gave a set each to Boney and Squeak. She twisted a pair between her fingers and inserted them in her ears, then suggested they do the same. "For the humming," she explained, addressing the confused looks on Boney and Squeak's faces. "If this is some kind of mind-altering frequency, we don't want it to control our thoughts or actions."

"Yes, of course," Squeak agreed, inserting the sponge plugs into his ears.

"Of course," Boney mimicked him, doing the same.

Samantha pointed to her eyes, then pointed to one of the windows along the length of the building, indicating that she'd like to take a look inside. Boney and Squeak nodded.

The three investigators spidered along the ground, eyes wary. When they reached the building, they wormed their way up to the window until they were staring through the glass.

Inside, the building was entirely white, except for a blue glow that emanated from the chute of what appeared to be a giant, space-age stainless steel dough-nut maker standing to one side of the room. The machine was big and square, with some kind of strange lettering etched over the surface. A conveyor belt rolled from beneath the chute to a point halfway across the room. Lockers made from the same shiny metal lined the walls.

All at once, the blue light from the machine began to flash and waver. The chute quivered and shook, the blue light flaring as a creature covered in an opaque, sticky ooze was spit from the machine onto the conveyor. It had a tangled mop of red hair and was wearing a Superman T-shirt and jeans.

"It's Itchy!" Boney shouted over the humming. "What have they done to him?"

"It's not Itchy!" Samantha yelled.

The conveyor continued to roll, the creature convulsing and clawing at the air as it struggled to life. At the end of the conveyor, the oozy thing tumbled to the floor, shuddering and shivering, the sticky film covering its body beginning to dry. The creature staggered in an attempt to stand, then looked around, dazed, its dark, expressionless eyes blinking against the cold, blue light.

"It *is* Itchy!" Boney hollered. He began pounding on the window. "Itchy! Over here! We've come to help you!"

Samantha grabbed Boney's hands. "I told you, it's not Itchy!"

The creature slowly turned its empty eyes toward Boney. Raising its arm, it pointed, menacing and vacant, then dropped its jaw and emitted a terrifying shriek. An alarm began to blare, and, in an instant, the doors of the shiny steel lockers burst open, revealing hundreds of red-haired clones.

"Oh crap," Squeak said.

CHAPTER ELEVEN

THE DISRUPTOR

"We have to get out of here—now!" Samantha said.

A high-pitched whistle shrilled, and the Itchy clones jolted to life as though struck through by a bolt of electricity. Together they pointed at the window where Squeak and Boney stood, then began shrieking as they swarmed from the building.

"Run!" Samantha shouted, dashing down the path toward the tracks.

Boney darted after her, his arms and legs pumping like pistons.

"Hey, wait up!" Squeak yelled, his messenger bag pounding against his legs as he flailed along the path.

The hordes of Itchy clones surged after them, demonic mouths gaping, the ground shaking from the impact of their feet.

"They're too fast!" Squeak wailed.

"Keep running!" Boney screamed.

Ahead of them, Samantha skidded to a stop and began digging through her bag. She pulled out a little black box with a big red button and held it up. "Come on!" she yelled to Boney and Squeak. "Don't look back!" She waved them on, and the two boys raced down the path with all their might.

Boney glimpsed over his shoulder and saw the tide of Itchys swelling and rising behind him. "They're gaining on us!"

"Run faster!" Samantha ordered.

Boney and Squeak streaked past her, running until they could see the train tracks at the edge of the woods. The boys turned just in time to see Samantha swallowed up by the wave of clones.

"She's gone!" Squeak cried.

All at once, a deep pulse shot through the air. It struck Boney and Squeak in the chest, knocking the wind from their lungs and sending them thumping to the ground. The clones sputtered and stalled, eyes lifeless, mouths opening and closing like confused goldfish. They gathered in a big ragged herd, bumping aimlessly into each other, little meeping noises emanating from their slack lips.

Squeak sat up, rubbing his head. "What happened?"

Boney looked at the listless clones. "They turned into zombies."

The Itchys began to slowly retreat, moving robotically in a line toward the warehouse. At the centre of the group stood Samantha, still holding the little black device in the air.

"Samantha!" Boney and Squeak called out. They scrambled up and ran to where she was standing.

"Are you okay?" Squeak asked.

Samantha continued holding the device in the air until the Itchys were out of sight, then shoved it into her bag. "I'm fine," she said.

Squeak turned to Boney. "What part of 'it's not Itchy' didn't you understand?"

"I'm sorry," Boney said, removing his earplugs. "I freaked out."

"I'll say."

"I'm fine," Samantha repeated, as though getting swarmed by clones was a daily event.

"What was that device you used?" Squeak asked in a loud voice.

Samantha removed the sponge plugs from her ears and pulled the little black box from her bag. "I call it the Disruptor."

"What?" Squeak said.

Samantha pointed to her ears, signalling to Squeak to remove his earplugs.

But Squeak just stared back like a quizzical mouse. "That's not the sort of thing one finds in a store."

Boney nudged him in the ribs. "Take your earplugs out."

"Huh?"

"Your earplugs!" Boney yelled. "Take them out!"

"Oh, right." Squeak flushed as he pulled the plugs from his ears, stuffing them into his pants pocket. He cleared his throat, speaking in a normal voice. "I said that's not the sort of thing you buy in a store. Did you build it?"

"Yes." Samantha handed the device to Squeak so he could take a closer look.

"How does it work?" Boney asked.

"It emits pulses that interfere with alien frequencies."

Boney pulled on his chin as he considered this. "How did you know we'd be dealing with aliens here? For all we knew, this could have been some kind of secret government project."

"What are you implying?" Samantha placed her hands on her hips.

Squeak shot Boney an irritated look. "Obviously, she did her research and came prepared — not like some people I know." He turned his back on his friend and examined the Disruptor. "Impressive piece of work." He handed the device back to Samantha, who replaced it in her bag.

"It's just a prototype," she said.

Boney stepped onto the train rail and began balancing his way toward home, Squeak and Samantha walking beside him. "So . . . you knew about the warehouse and the . . . um . . ." He snapped his fingers, searching for the right word.

"Clones," Samantha said. "I believe that's the word you're looking for."

"Clones," Squeak echoed. He paused. "How strange they should decide to reproduce Itchy . . ."

"Who's 'they'?" Boney asked.

"The aliens," Squeak said, as though it were common knowledge now.

Samantha tossed her hair. "It may not be as strange as you think. They usually look for . . . impressionable personalities to do their work."

Boney turned to her. "Are you saying Itchy's dumb?"

Samantha stared at him. "I didn't say that."

"She didn't say that," Squeak jumped in.

"They just find it easier to work with *suggestible* types," Samantha said.

Boney frowned. "How do you know all this? And who are *they*, exactly?" He stepped off the tracks and pushed through the bushes into his backyard. "What could they possibly hope to achieve by cloning Itchy? He may not be the brightest crayon in the box, but he would never do anything to hurt anyone."

Squeak squeezed through the bushes after Boney. "Why did the clones chase us then?"

"They've likely been programmed to respond to threatening situations," Samantha said, following Squeak through the hole in the hedge. "When they saw Boney banging on the window, they probably perceived him as a threat to the safety of their project and attacked."

Boney shook his head. "I don't get it. What good is it to send a giant group of clones out in the world to do your bidding? They'll just get caught."

"They don't go around in a group. They hunt alone to avoid suspicion." Samantha reached into her bag and pulled out a copy of the local newspaper as proof, flapping it open to the photo of the Itchy clone stealing the doughnuts. "See . . . only one clone caught on camera."

Squeak considered the photo. "What about the police? They were looking for Itchy earlier."

Samantha nodded. "They caught him."

"What?"

"Not Itchy," Samantha said. "One of the clones. I saw them grab it when I was running toward the train

tracks. It put up a big fight, but they managed to hand-
cuff it and get it in the cruiser."

"What's going to happen to it?" Boney asked.

"They'll probably put it in jail." Samantha tucked
her hair behind her ears.

Boney's shoulders slumped. "This is so crazy." He
kicked a stone as he walked to the ladder at the base of
the oak tree.

Squeak pointed to a sign newly affixed to the side of
the clubhouse. "Uhhh . . . what's that?"

Boney and Samantha stared at the sign. The words
were painted in big black letters.

"No girls allowed," Samantha read.

"Oh." Boney scratched his head and gave a nervous
little laugh. "I guess Itchy must have put that there."

Squeak stiffened. "We never agreed on this new
initiative."

"I think this is the least of our worries," Boney said.

Squeak became animated. "But the Order of Odd
Fellows is a democracy. We always vote on such
motions. We can't have members just doing whatever
they want."

"What's the Order of Odd Fellows?" Samantha asked.

Boney's face flushed. "Oh, it's . . . um . . . a group that
we belong to."

"It's our club," Squeak said. "We established it years

ago. I even wrote a chant." He raised his fist in the air. "We are weird, we are here, get used to it!"

Boney pushed Squeak's arm down. "Uhhh . . . yeah . . ."

Samantha studied Boney with amusement. "I like it."

Boney waved at the sign as a diversionary tactic. "How do we even know the real Itchy did this? There are millions of Itchys in that warehouse out there. Who knows what they're up to?"

Samantha gave him a wry smile. "I don't think they're concerned about girls in your clubhouse."

Boney clenched his jaw. "Well, why don't you tell us what's going on? You seem to know a lot."

"Gladly. But I'd rather not loiter out in the open." Samantha looked over her shoulder.

Boney took the hint. He gestured at the ladder. Samantha put her hands on the rungs and was about to climb when Squeak stopped her.

"You'd better let me go first. We have no idea who could be up there."

Boney gave him a look. "Aren't you the gentleman."

Squeak brushed him off and began climbing the ladder. When he reached the top he stuck his head through the opening and looked around. "It's safe. Nobody but Henry up here."

"Thanks, Tarzan," Boney called back. He allowed Samantha to climb next, then followed several rungs behind.

Squeak was already sitting at the table when Boney pulled himself into the clubhouse. Samantha took the seat next to Squeak.

"Just for the record, what *were* you doing up here with Itchy earlier?" Boney asked.

"It wasn't Itchy," Samantha said. "It was one of them."

Squeak's eyes widened. "So our security has been breached."

"Not entirely." Samantha looked at Henry, who cocked his head in her direction. "It seems your leghorn can tell the difference."

Squeak's face lit up. "Really?"

Samantha nodded. "I was hoping to speak to you about the . . . situation . . . when one of the clones followed me here. Henry recognized it wasn't Itchy right away and chased it down the ladder."

Squeak smiled his gap-toothed smile. "Good boy!" he praised the rooster.

Henry raised his head and fluffed his feathers proudly.

Boney sat at the table. "Did you notice how quick those clones are? It's like they're supercharged or something."

"Did you notice their eyes?" Squeak said. "They're vacant, like a doll's eyes. They look possessed."

Samantha grew quiet, the sunlight dappling across her face through the clubhouse window. "I've never had a close encounter with a clone before," she confessed. "I was actually really scared when they swarmed me."

"So were we," Squeak admitted. "We thought you were a goner."

Boney nodded soberly. He pulled thoughtfully on his long chin. "Not to push the issue or anything . . . but how did you know about the situation?"

Samantha started to speak, and then raised her finger to her lips. "What's that noise?"

There was a rustling sound at the base of the ladder. Boney, Squeak, and Samantha froze in their seats, their startled faces turned toward Escape Hatch #1. They could hear the distinct sound of something climbing the rungs toward the clubhouse. And then a tangled mop of red hair popped through the hole. The creature rose to full height, teeth bared like a rabid dog.

CHAPTER TWELVE

SPACE INVADERS

Boney, Squeak, and Samantha screamed at the top of their lungs.

Henry charged the monster, wings beating. He flew toward its face, but then dropped like a stone, a familiar glint in his yellow eyes.

"What the heck is wrong with everybody?" the intruder said. He reached for the rooster and scratched him on the neck.

"Itchy!" Boney shouted with relief. "Why were you sneaking up on us?"

"I wasn't sneaking up on anyone," Itchy said. "I just thought we could play with the new batch of kittens." He pulled a basket of kittens from behind his back and gave a big sneeze.

Samantha's face brightened. "Kittens!"

"So you're not mad at us anymore?" Squeak asked.

Itchy pulled out a hanky and blew his nose. "What's she doing here?" He glowered at Samantha. "Didn't you read the sign? NO GIRLS ALLOWED. And you're sitting in my chair."

"Oh." Samantha lowered her eyes.

Boney stood up from the table. "Yeah, we need to talk to you about that."

"We didn't vote on it," Squeak said.

Itchy sniffed. "What's there to talk about?"

"A lot," Samantha said.

Itchy brandished his hanky. "See—she's taking over already."

"We need her help," Squeak said. "There's something terrible going on."

Itchy scoffed. "I'll say."

Samantha retrieved a file folder from her bag and flipped it open. It was filled with photographs. She placed the snapshots in chronological order across the table.

Itchy rushed over. "Hey, that's us in those pictures! Where'd you get these?"

"I took them the day before the Flying Fiends Amateur Aircraft Competition," Samantha said.

The Odds stared at the photos, mouths open. The pictures showed a huge saucer-shaped craft hovering over the three boys as they stood on Starky Hill, wide-eyed and frozen in place, the dust whirling around.

Itchy choked. "Is that a . . . spaceship?"

The three boys exchanged terrified looks.

"This explains the missing time," Squeak said.

Samantha tapped her watch. "Twenty minutes. The spaceship probed you with that beam of light, stealing samples of your DNA. They used the information to clone Itchy."

Itchy's face turned white as a sheet. "What do you mean '*clone*'?"

Samantha looked to Boney and Squeak for help.

Boney hesitated before he spoke. "There are hundreds of you out there."

Itchy's face grew paler still. "What are you talking about?"

"It's true," Squeak said. "There's this place in the woods — it's like a giant warehouse. They're using some kind of positronic light technology to clone full-scale copies of you . . ." His voice trailed off at the end.

Itchy withered into Boney's chair at the table. "I feel sick."

Boney pulled the crumpled newspaper photo from his pocket. He smoothed out the picture and placed it in front of Itchy. "Your clones are running amok. They're looting and causing all kinds of trouble."

"The police came this morning," Samantha added.

"The police!" Itchy blurted.

Samantha nodded. "They managed to catch one of your clones."

Itchy searched his friends' faces. Boney stared back sympathetically. Squeak bit his nails. "I knew something strange happened that night. I just couldn't ascertain what it was exactly."

Itchy groaned, placing the basket of kittens on the table. Boney turned to Samantha.

"How did you know the spaceship would be at Starky Hill that day?"

Samantha pulled a magazine from her bag and tossed it in front of the boys. The cover showed a tornado twisting through a barren landscape; the name STORM CHASER was sprayed across the top of the magazine in big yellow letters.

Squeak picked up the magazine and flipped through the pages. "I know this publication. I was considering getting a subscription."

"What do tornadoes have to do with aliens?" Boney asked.

"The electrical anomaly we experienced the other night," Squeak said, pushing on the bridge of his goggles. "It's been theorized that alien aircraft create both electrical and meteorological occurrences when they travel, as a result of their propulsion technology."

"And as a means of avoiding detection," Samantha said.

Boney pulled on his chin. "So . . . the occurrences act as a kind of stormy camouflage . . ."

"Exactly. That storm the other night tipped me off. So I used my electro-node-a-metre to detect fluctuations in the atmosphere." Samantha retrieved the wandlike instrument from her bag and held it up. "And it led me straight to Starky Hill."

"Where you saw us," Boney said.

"Yes."

Squeak smiled. "So . . . you weren't spying on us."

Samantha looked confused. "No . . . Why would I be spying on you?"

Squeak shrugged. "Oh . . . no reason." He made a self-satisfied face at Boney and Itchy, then reached for the electro-node-a-metre. "Do you mind if I look at it?"

"Not at all." Samantha handed him the device. "I got the schematics from an earlier issue of *Storm Chaser*— volume twelve. I modified it slightly for my purposes, but the basic principle is the same."

Squeak engaged the switch and the electro-node-a-metre started to hum, the thin wire arms rising and slowly whirling like a propeller. "It's quite similar to the Apparator in purpose," he observed.

Samantha raised an eyebrow. "The Apparator . . . ?"

Squeak flipped the switch off. "The ghost detector that I—or should I say we—developed." He gestured toward Boney and Itchy. "It won the Invention Convention at our school."

"Congratulations," Samantha said.

"What has any of this got to do with spaceships?!" Itchy demanded.

Squeak patted him gently on the back. "It's quite simple. The electro-node-a-metre registered the electronic signature of the alien vessel, leading Samantha—"

"Please, call me Sam."

"Leading *Sam* to Starky Hill—which is why she was able to take pictures of us while we were being scanned for DNA by the alien craft."

Itchy let out an involuntary sob. "But why? Why would they want to clone me? Who are these people?"

"Not people," Sam said. "Extraterrestrials."

Boney clenched his jaw. "Aliens."

Itchy's face drained to the colour of spoiled milk. "Little green men. I hate those guys."

"Actually, they're grey," Sam quietly corrected him.

"You've seen them?" Boney and Squeak asked.

"I've seen pictures. Fourth-level Greys—the ones responsible for abducting human beings."

Itchy snivelled, his hands on either side of his head. "What do you mean '*the ones responsible for abducting human beings*'? There's more than one kind of alien?"

"Of course." Sam pushed her hair behind her ears.

"There are at least twenty-three species of extraterrestrials visiting our planet at this time . . . at least . . . that's what the literature purports."

"How do you know all this stuff?" Boney asked.

Sam grew wistful. "My father is an astrophysicist. He was one of the founding members of SETI."

"Search for Extraterrestrial Intelligence?!" Squeak exclaimed. "How cool is that!"

Boney placed his hand on Squeak's shoulder. "Calm down, Mr. Spock."

"But this is incredible!" Squeak said. "I'd *love* to meet your father! I have so many questions."

Itchy clutched his stomach. "I think I'm going to throw up . . ."

"Is your mother a scientist as well?" Squeak asked Sam. "I'd love to meet her, too."

A flicker of sadness crossed Sam's eyes before she lowered them. "My mother's gone. She disappeared when I was a baby, in a failed teleportation experiment conducted by my father. He's never forgiven himself. He's pretty much a recluse now."

Boney and Squeak shifted in their sneakers while Itchy continued to sniff and blubber incoherently at the table. After several excruciating moments, Boney broke the silence.

"I'm sorry. My parents disappeared when I was

just a baby, too—in a ballooning accident. I don't really remember a lot about them."

Sam raised her eyes. "Well, Father and I are making a new start. We moved here to get away from old memories."

"It's not such a bad place," Squeak said. "Despite the clone crisis we're currently facing . . ."

This made Itchy moan even louder. Boney ran his hand through his hair. "What I want to know is what the aliens expect to accomplish with thousands of Itchys. I mean . . . *we* know he's great . . . but does the rest of the universe . . . ?"

Boney, Squeak, and Sam turned to where Itchy sat, his bottom lip quivering uncontrollably, his eyebrows crumpled across his drawn, white face. He blew his nose loudly several times, sniffing and snorting noisily as he fumbled and folded his old hanky with each blow. He raised his mournful face to his friends, his eyes blinking wildly. "What are we going to do?"

Squeak took a box of saltines off the shelf and handed it to Itchy. "Here. Have these. It always makes you feel better when you eat."

Itchy shook his head, refusing the crackers. Squeak shot Boney a worried look.

"You know what this means, don't you?" Boney said. "It means the vampire my aunt saw staring through our kitchen window was an Itchy clone."

Itchy's head popped up. "What vampire?"

"They know where we live," Squeak murmured.

"What vampire?" Itchy whimpered. "Will someone please tell me what's going on?"

Sam bit her lower lip. "They know everything about you, I imagine."

Itchy groaned louder still. "What have I ever done to them?" He dropped his forehead to the table. The kittens scrambled from their basket and began pawing at his bramble-bush hair, purring loudly. Itchy gathered them in his arms and held them to his face. "It's all so terrible. Why is this happening to me?"

"What could the aliens possibly want from us?" Boney asked.

Sam pulled her notebook from her bag and flipped through several pages. "Historically, aliens have visited earth to create alien-human hybrids."

"With someone like Itchy?" Boney blurted out.

Itchy sneezed and blew his nose again with a big honk.

Squeak pulled his notebook from his messenger bag. "They've also been reported to be mining for resources similar to those squandered on their own planets."

Boney snapped his fingers. "Or maybe they're here because they want to eat people, like we saw on that *Twilight Zone* episode."

"Ahhh!" Itchy cried out, rocking his head from side to side on the table, the kittens still poking and clawing playfully at his hair.

Squeak made a face at Boney. Boney shrugged apologetically.

"Well, whatever the reason, we're going to find out what they intend to do," Sam vowed. "And we won't let anything happen to Itchy."

Itchy raised his head, snorting fitfully. "Really?"

"Of course not," Sam reassured him. She looked to Boney and Squeak for support.

"No, of course not," Squeak and Boney said. "We won't let anything happen to you."

"We know where their warehouse is," Boney offered hopefully. "That's a start."

"Now we need to find the Mother Ship," Sam said. "From what I've read, the ship shouldn't be too far from the warehouse. In fact, usually it's cloaked and hovering very close by."

"Why do they need a warehouse for the clones if they have a spaceship?" Boney asked.

"It's part of their deception," Squeak explained. "That way, if the clones get caught, they can't be traced back to the spacecraft."

"Well, we're going to beat them at their own game."

Boney smacked his fist into the palm of his hand. "We'll find the Mother Ship and destroy the Itchys."

Itchy looked up in horror. "But . . . how will we tell the difference between the fake Itchys and the real me?"

There was silence in the clubhouse as Boney, Squeak, and Sam considered this challenge. Itchy panicked, grabbing Squeak's arm, his voice breaking on hysteria. "Can't you just invent something?"

Squeak pried Itchy's hand away. "We really don't have time."

"No, we don't," Sam solemnly agreed.

"I'm doomed!" Itchy wailed.

But then Sam's face suddenly brightened. "I have an idea!"

Chapter Thirteen

Animal Companions

Sam jumped up from the table, her eyes glittering with excitement. "We can use Henry to determine who the clones are! He knew instantly that the Itchy clone in the clubhouse was a fake."

"And the kittens," Boney said. "Somehow, they knew the difference, too. They hissed at that clone at the Flying Fiends Competition. I knew there was something funny going on there."

Itchy's face screwed up as though he'd just swallowed a fly. "There was a clone at the competition?"

"Yes," Boney said. "Remember when I sent you to get lemonade?"

"Yeah . . ."

"Well, you returned empty-handed—at least, the clone did—and I thought it was you. It was wearing my

Superman T-shirt and I thought you'd changed because you were too embarrassed to wear the pink kitten shirt your mom made."

Itchy wiped his nose. "What did it want?"

"I don't know. It just stood there, staring blankly, until I yelled at it to go get lemonade and it left."

"That falls within the realm of normalcy," Squeak observed.

Boney nodded. "That's why I didn't suspect anything. But the kittens knew there was something wrong because they began to hiss and growl the second it showed up."

Itchy's eyes glimmered hopefully. "So . . . all we have to do is carry kittens everywhere we go . . . ?"

"Yes!" Boney said.

Sam took a kitten from Itchy's arms. "I like this one with the black and white spots." She held the kitten up to her face. "I'm going to call him Fluffy." And then she started speaking in a strange, high-pitched voice. "Isn't he just the cutest thing on the planet? Isn't he just the sweetest, fluffiest, lovey-dovey boy? Yes, he is! He's a lovey-dovey boy!" She squealed and hugged the kitten, kissing him over and over.

The boys stared at each other uncomfortably.

"Disgusting," Itchy muttered.

"I'm rather fond of the orange one," Squeak piped up, taking the orange kitten from Itchy.

"And . . . uh . . . I really like this striped grey one," Boney said, claiming the last kitten.

Squeak looked at Boney, raising an eyebrow and speaking in his best Mr. Spock voice. "Your aunt's response to the kitten should prove most interesting."

"What do you mean?" Boney asked.

Squeak continued to stare at him, eyebrow pitched. "Do you really think she's going to allow you to have a cat?"

"I'll have to come up with a reason that my aunt can't refuse."

"No one can guarantee the actions of another," Squeak said.

Boney shrugged. "My aunt's pretty predictable."

"True. Assuming she does allow you to keep the kitten, what do you intend on calling him?"

Boney considered the kitten for a moment. "I think Tiger's a good name for a striped cat. How about you? What will you call your kitten? Leonardo da Vinci?"

"That would be illogical. He looks more like a Spock to me."

"Of course," Boney said. "It's the ears."

"What about Itchy?" Sam asked. "He doesn't have a kitten."

Itchy waved his dirty hanky. "Oh, don't worry about me. My house is crawling with cats. Besides, I think I'm allergic." He sneezed loudly.

"How about Henry?" Boney suggested. "You're not allergic to him."

The friends turned to look at the rooster, who was slumbering on the clubhouse floor, his head under his wing. He seemed to sense he was being watched and startled awake, shaking his feathers and blinking a yellow eye in Itchy's direction.

Boney smiled. "See? He knows we're talking about him. He'll keep you safe from the clones, Itchy."

Itchy held out his hand. The rooster strutted over and hopped into his lap, nestling in.

"Perfect," Boney said. "Now all we need is an action plan." He turned to Sam. "You seem to know more about this than any of us. What would you suggest?"

Sam held Fluffy up to her face as the kitten purred loudly. "I think we should go back to the warehouse in the woods and try to find the Mother Ship. Once we accomplish that, we can find out who we're dealing with and what exactly it is that they want."

"Affirmative," Squeak said.

"Then what?" Boney asked.

Sam thought about it for a moment. "I guess we have no choice but to play it by ear. We really don't know what we're up against at this point."

Itchy slumped in his chair. "Oh great. We're doomed."

"We're not doomed," Sam said. "I have the Disruptor. And we have Henry and the kittens."

Squeak adjusted his goggles. "They should prove valuable."

"Definitely," Boney agreed. He was just about to elaborate when his aunt called out the kitchen window.

"Boneeey! Suppertime!"

Boney groaned. "Gotta go, guys. But we can meet up after supper. I'll call you on the Tele-tube."

"What's the Tele-tube?" Sam asked.

"It's a primitive form of communication," Squeak answered.

"But it works," Boney said. "We speak to each other through plastic tubes so our parents won't hear us."

Sam tossed her hair. "That's interesting."

"Boneeey!" his aunt called again.

Boney rolled his eyes. "Okay, I've really got to go before my aunt comes out here. Just in case, let's plan to meet in the clubhouse tomorrow morning at eight—sharp."

Squeak saluted. "In full regalia?"

Boney saluted back. "Full regalia. And if anybody sees

or hears anything out of the ordinary before then, transmit over the Tele-tube. Sam, you can't do that, obviously, so we'll just have to wait for your report when we meet next."

"Unless it's urgent," Squeak said. "Then you could just throw a rock at my bedroom window . . . or something."

"Right," Boney said.

Itchy sniffed. "Do you think it's safe for Henry to stay in the clubhouse alone?"

"He'll be fine," Boney assured him.

"But what if the clones come to get him?"

Boney raised one of Henry's legs, showing off his long rooster spurs. "I don't think those clones will be coming back here anytime soon. Henry gave that last one quite the scare."

"It's true," Sam said. "That clone practically flew down the ladder with Henry on its back."

Itchy smiled half-heartedly. He pulled some cornmeal from his pocket and scattered it for Henry on the clubhouse floor. "I guess he should be okay."

"William Boneham!" Boney's aunt shrieked. "Supper is ready!"

Squeak patted Boney on the shoulder. "Good luck with the kitten." He placed Spock in his messenger bag and slipped down the fire pole in Escape Hatch #2.

"Talk to you later," Sam said, clutching her kitten and following Squeak down the pole.

Itchy just waved his hanky and zipped down the pole with the empty kitten basket. Boney streaked after him, Tiger tucked under one arm.

CHAPTER FOURTEEN

TUMMY TROUBLES

Boney spied through the kitchen window before entering the house. His uncle was sitting at the table, reading the paper, a big hole in the front page where Boney had ripped out the picture of the Itchy clone. His aunt was fussing about, rattling some pans on the stove. Boney gazed at the kitten purring in his arms. He knew his uncle would let him keep the pet, but his aunt was another story. She wouldn't allow the kitten to stay unless he came up with a very good reason, which he didn't have the energy to do at the moment.

"I'll just hide you for the time being," Boney said, tucking the kitten under his T-shirt and folding his hands casually across the resulting bump on his stomach. He turned the knob on the door, and then refolded his hands over the bump as he stepped into the house.

"It's about time, young man!" his aunt scolded

immediately. "I practically screamed myself hoarse calling for you."

"Yes, Auntie." Boney turned his back to her as she continued her tirade. He tried to conceal the kitten while pushing his sneakers off with his feet. But his aunt wasn't that easily fooled.

"What have you got there?" She sniffed, walking toward him.

"Nothing."

"Why are you clutching your stomach?"

Boney froze. "I don't feel well."

His aunt leaned in to take a closer look. "Your stomach looks all bloated. Do you have a fever? Let me feel your forehead."

Boney jumped back. "NO! It's okay. I just have to go to the washroom really badly." He hopped lightly from foot to foot to show his distress. The kitten began to squirm beneath his shirt.

His aunt stared in horror at the wiggling lump. "Good heavens!" She turned to Boney's uncle. "Robert, get the ipecac. I think William has worms."

"It's not worms," Boney said. "I just need to go to the washroom."

"Don't move," his aunt ordered. She rummaged through the cupboards until she found the bottle of medicine she was looking for, and then she got a tablespoon from the cutlery drawer. Unscrewing the cap on the bottle, she walked toward Boney, filling the spoon with gruesome yellow liquid.

Boney grimaced, struggling to contain the squirming kitten. "Really, Auntie, I'm okay—I think it's just food poisoning."

His aunt recoiled as though bitten. "Food poisoning? Not from this kitchen." She turned to her husband. "Robert? How's your stomach?"

"Huh?" Boney's uncle sputtered through his moustache, fluttering his newspaper absently.

"Maybe I got it from something I ate at the clubhouse," Boney said, the kitten becoming more and more agitated.

"Well, it won't hurt you to take a little medicine." His aunt raised the spoon of jiggling syrup.

Boney jerked away from the spoon. "Auntie, please!" he howled, the kitten screeching from his shirt and landing between his feet with a loud plop!

The sight of the kitten caused his aunt to shriek and faint. She collapsed on the kitchen floor, the ipecac syrup fanning from the bottle in a putrid yellow arc across the room.

Boney's uncle leaped to his feet and trampled through the sticky syrup, leaving yellow footprints across the linoleum. He knelt at his wife's side, flapping his folded newspaper in her face. Boney grabbed the terrified kitten and held him to his chest.

"Can I keep him, Uncle?" he begged. "I promise I'll take care of him. You won't even have to pay for food or anything."

Boney's uncle continued to fan his wife with the newspaper. "You'd better take that kitten up to your room," he ordered. "We'll discuss this in the morning — once your aunt has had a chance to recover."

Boney rushed upstairs with the kitten. He could hear his uncle helping his aunt up the stairs, her wails echoing through the house. He waited until things settled down, then searched his room for an old cardboard box for the kitten's litter, cutting the edges down to the proper height. When he was sure his aunt was safely stowed in her bed, Boney snuck downstairs with the makeshift litter box and crept outside to get some soil from the rose garden. Looking over his shoulder for clones, Boney quickly filled the box with his hands, brushing them off on his jeans before sneaking back into the house.

In the kitchen, the table was still set for dinner, pots and pans abandoned on the stove. His aunt had never been this upset before. He would never hear the end of it. Desperate to make amends, Boney grabbed the dish-cloth from the sink and furiously scrubbed the yellow ipecac syrup from the floor, rinsing the cloth several times until the kitchen was clean. As he replaced the cloth in the sink, Boney's stomach growled loudly. Despite everything, he was hungry. He cautiously peeked into the pots: Brussels sprouts and one of his aunt's famous soup-can recipes. Boney screwed up his face at the sprouts, slapping the lid back on the pot. He found a fork in the cutlery drawer and began wolfing down big mouthfuls of casserole, barely chewing between bites.

When he was satisfied, he covered the pot and got a cereal bowl from the cupboard. After filling the bowl with milk, Boney quietly took it and the litter box upstairs for Tiger. The kitten sniffed at the bowl and began lapping the milk. Boney sat back, rubbing his forehead.

Squeak called over the Tele-tube. "Are you there, Boney? Over."

Boney uncovered the tube. "Boney here."

"Just wondering how your aunt received the kitten," Squeak said.

"She fainted."

"What? What happened?"

Boney rested his chin in his hand. "I tried to hide Tiger under my shirt, but he squirmed and fell out. I guess my aunt was . . . surprised."

"Oh. I see."

"She thought I had worms," Boney explained. "She tried to give me ipecac."

Squeak stared at Boney from his bedroom window. "Ipecac? Isn't that an emetic?"

"What do you mean?"

Squeak made a barfing sound through the tube. "It's used to make people throw up."

Boney winced. "Yeah. There was no way I was going to take it."

"Why would your aunt think that was a good idea?" Squeak wondered. "I've never heard of using ipecac for worms before . . ."

"Who knows? She probably read it in one of her women's magazines."

"Fascinating," Squeak said. "I'm assuming you're grounded?"

Boney saluted. "Roger that. I'm in for the night. But what about you? Is your dad going to let you keep Spock?"

"Unknown. He's working late, as usual."

"Ah."

The tube fell silent.

"Boney . . ." Squeak finally spoke. "Do you think we'll be able to solve this clone problem?"

Boney rubbed his chin. "I don't know. But I hope so."

There was another pause before Squeak spoke again. "Sam is pretty cool, isn't she?"

"Yeah . . . she's smart. Almost as smart as you."

"Smarter, I think," Squeak confessed.

"I don't know if that's possible."

"She beat me at the Flying Fiends Competition."

"You didn't know her entry would be armed and dangerous," Boney said.

"It wouldn't have made a difference," Squeak said. "I was losing anyway."

"Well—" Boney started to speak, but there was a sharp rap on his bedroom door.

"Get to bed," his uncle commanded.

"Gotta go," Boney whispered. He threw the towel over the end of the Tele-tube and picked Tiger up, holding the kitten in the air for Squeak to see. Squeak nodded and held his kitten up as well. "Eight a.m.," Boney mouthed.

"Eight a.m." Squeak's voice floated through the tube.

Chapter Fifteen

Intruders!

With nothing to entertain him, Boney changed into his pyjamas and climbed into bed, placing Tiger next to him. The kitten curled on top of the blanket and began purring loudly. Boney's eyelids grew heavier and heavier, the kitten's purring lulling him deeper and deeper. He drifted off to sleep, only to be woken several hours later by the sound of the kitten hissing and growling ferociously at the foot of the bed. Boney jerked awake, just in time to hear his bedroom window slowly scraping open.

His voice quavered through the dark. "Who's there?"

The sash flung open with a bang, and a tangled mass of red hair popped in.

"AaaaaAAAAhhhhhaaAAAAhhhhHH!" Boney screamed as the demonic white face of an Itchy clone snapped into view. Jumping up, Boney grabbed the pillow from his bed. He swung it like a Viking, hitting the clone over and over as he yelled at the top of his lungs, "Get out of here, you red-headed freak!"

The clone clawed at the pillow, trying to wrench it from Boney's hands. Boney swung wildly, knocking the clone's head from side to side like a punching bag. The clone scrabbled to get in the room and was nearly through the window when Tiger launched himself from the end of the bed. The kitten flew through the air and landed in the clone's hair, snarling and scratching like an enraged wildcat. The clone shrieked and waved its hands, trying to pull the hissing kitten off its head. It lost its footing and fell back, the kitten jumping safely into the room as the clone crashed to the ground.

There was a loud knock on the bedroom door. "What's going on in there?" Boney's uncle demanded.

"Nothing," Boney called back, his voice shaking. "Just a bad dream. I'm fine now."

There was the sound of shuffling outside the door, and then the hall grew quiet. Boney pushed the window shut and engaged the lock, his chest still heaving as he peered through the glass at the clone lying scrambled on the ground. But the creature rose, as though pulled by strings, like a marionette, and stood glaring at Boney, its horrible face a pale spectre in the night. It was soon joined by another clone, and then another and another, until a dozen white faces glared up at his bedroom window. Boney watched in terror as the clones moved in unison toward the rose trellis on the wall of the house. They were just about to start climbing when a whistle pierced the darkness. The clones turned as one, marched from the yard, and were gone.

Boney collapsed on the end of his bed, Tiger slinking around his feet. He reached down, picked the kitten up, and hugged him. "You saved my life," he whispered into the kitten's fur. Hands trembling, Boney raised the Tele-tube to his lips. "Are you there, Squeak? Over." He waited a few seconds and then leaned toward the Teletube again. "Come in, Squeak, it's urgent. Over."

Nothing. Boney threw the Tele-tube down and covered it with the towel. He rechecked the lock on the window and then stared down through the glass one more time, convinced the clones would reappear.

But the yard was empty. A shiver ran up Boney's spine. What if the clones were trying to get in through another window in the house? And just how many were out there?

Kitten in hand, Boney slowly opened the door to his room and crept out. He stood in the dark at the top of the stairs, listening. The house was unusually quiet. He began walking down the stairs, hesitating with each step as he scanned for alien marauders. When he reached the landing at the bottom, he paused again.

Heart racing, he checked and double-checked the locks on the front door. Then he slunk through the rest of the house, hiding behind chairs and curtains before testing the locks on the windows and doors to make sure everything was secure.

When he was positive there were no more clones trying to break in, Boney crept back upstairs with the kitten and closed his bedroom door behind him. Fastening the lock on his window a third time, he finally climbed into bed. He lay there, too frightened to sleep, glancing at his alarm clock every few minutes. It seemed the faster his mind whirled, the slower time crawled, until he picked up the clock and held it to his ear, convinced it had stopped ticking altogether.

The kitten didn't seem to care about clones, though. He was curled up on the blanket as before, his head tucked neatly into his tail. Boney wished he could be so relaxed. He wished he had a jawbreaker, too, but he was too afraid to get out of bed to search for one in the sock drawer of his dresser. Despite the overwhelming heat in his room, he pulled the sheet up under his chin, watching as the small metal fan on his desk whirled languidly from side to side. He could barely breathe, but he wasn't about to open his window for fear the clone would show up. So there was nothing to do but lie there, wondering why Squeak hadn't answered his

call over the Tele-tube. Boney's mind began to race,
spinning frightful scenarios in which the clones had
captured and tortured his friends. This held him cap-
tive for a bleary-eyed hour until exhaustion overcame
him and he fell into a fitful sleep.

CHAPTER SIXTEEN

KITTEN AROUND

Boney woke with a start to the sound of his aunt's voice hollering up the stairs.

"William Boneham! Get down here this instant!"

Kicking the sheet off his legs, Boney sprang out of bed, careful to avoid the kitten. But Tiger was already up, exploring the room. He'd found a marble under the dresser and was happily batting it back and forth, scrabbling noisily after it when it escaped his paws.

Boney checked his clock. Seven-twenty-nine. He would need to hurry if he was going to be on time for the eight a.m. rendezvous at the clubhouse. Retrieving a box from under his bed, he opened it. Inside was a full set of camouflage army fatigues. He jumped into the fatigues, then pulled an olive-drab toque from the box and slipped it on his head. Next, he fished a pair of shiny black combat boots from under his bed and put them on, lacing them with practised precision. When he was finished, Boney walked over to his dresser and took a small tin from his sock drawer. Opening the tin, he smeared camouflage on his cheeks and forehead, taking a moment to admire himself in the mirror before replacing the tin in the drawer.

"William!" his aunt called again.

"You'd better stay here," Boney said to Tiger as he opened the door to his room. "Auntie is in no mood for antics."

But Tiger had other plans. He darted from the room and was padding merrily down the stairs, tail up, before Boney had a chance to stop him.

"Kitten!" Boney hissed.

Tiger slipped into the living room.

"Hey! Get back here!" Boney whispered.

Trotting carefully down the stairs, Boney chased the kitten into the kitchen where his aunt stood scowling, red gingham tea towel fixed over her arm.

"William Boneham," she started in. "You have some nerve bringing a cat into this house. I suppose you thought you could hide it?"

Tiger purred and smiled, rubbing himself against her legs. She tried to shoo the cat away with the gingham dish towel.

"I'm sorry—" Boney began to apologize, but his aunt cut him off.

"I have never had use for a cat in the past, nor will I in the future. I'm of a mind to—"

But her lecture ended with a sharp shriek when a moth flew out of nowhere and swooped drunkenly at her head. Whipping the tea towel into action, she screamed and hopped around like a terrified chimp, attacking the moth as though it were a venomous killer. In her terror, she stumbled over a kitchen chair, tumbling to the floor with a shout, her skinny legs kicking at the air, the gingham tea towel cracking like a bullwhip.

"It's just a moth!" Boney yelled. But he couldn't be heard over his aunt's cries, which were so hysterical his uncle came crashing into the room as if the house were on fire.

"What's going on here?" he blustered.

Boney's aunt screeched, "Get it, Robert, get it!"

All at once, the kitten sprang. He sailed across the kitchen like Pegasus, arcing over Boney's aunt and snagging the moth in mid-air with his front paws. Tucking into a ball, he rolled across the kitchen floor, eating the moth before sliding to a stop in front of the stove.

"Wow!" Boney shouted. "Did you see that?"

His aunt blinked from her position on the floor.

His uncle snuffled through his moustache. "Well, that takes care of that." He reached down and helped his rattled wife to her feet.

Boney picked Tiger up and beamed, putting on his most endearing face. "See how useful he is? Can we please keep him, pleeease?"

His aunt straightened her skirts and her hair, then folded the gingham tea towel over her arm. She cleared her throat and played with the button at the top of her blouse, her lips pinched. "Well . . . I suppose it wouldn't be too much trouble . . ."

"He's no trouble at all," Boney assured her. "And I'll pay for his food and everything."

"Fine," his aunt finally croaked. "But if I find him scratching at the furniture . . ."

"He won't, Auntie, I promise." Boney crossed his heart.

Boney's uncle stepped in. "He'll have to go to the vet."

"We can take him whenever you want," Boney said. He noticed the time. Seven-fifty-eight. He had two minutes to make his meeting at the clubhouse! "Uhhh . . . I have to go now. I'm late for a meeting . . . but we can talk about this later."

"What meeting?" his aunt asked. "And what about breakfast?"

"Gotta go!" Boney dashed out the door with the kitten. He raced to the bottom of the tree house, looking around for any suspicious activity before climbing the rope ladder. Slowly raising his head through Escape Hatch #1, Boney could see Henry sleeping peacefully in his box at the other end of the clubhouse. "Must be safe if Henry is okay," he said to Tiger as he climbed the rest of the way in.

Moments later, there was noise at the base of the tree. Boney looked out the window and saw Squeak and Sam climbing up the ladder with their kittens. Squeak's camouflaged face peeked through the escape hatch opening.

"It's okay," Boney said. "The coast is clear."

Squeak signalled to Sam, and the two pulled themselves up into the clubhouse. They were both dressed in full military style: boots, fatigues, toques, camo, and kitten clone-detectors. Sam held up a box of kitten chow and a shallow bowl.

"I brought food for our clone-detectors — and cat litter with a box." She placed her kitten on the clubhouse floor, arranged the litter box, and filled the bowl with chow.

The sound of the kibble woke Henry from his slumber. He cocked his head and eyed the food, jumped from his box, and ruffled his feathers. Boney and Squeak placed their kittens by the bowl. Henry swaggered over and gazed at the kittens, then pecked at the chow.

"That's so cute," Sam cooed. "I wish I had my camera."

Squeak pulled his Polaroid from his messenger bag. "I've got mine." He took a picture and handed the photo to Sam so she could watch it develop.

"You are sooo sweet!" Sam squealed.

A delirious giggle escaped from Squeak's lips, but he quickly composed himself when he saw the horrified look on Boney's face.

Sam grinned at the photo as the image emerged. But then she grew serious again. "Where's Itchy?"

Squeak sighed. "He's often late."

"Let's just hope he's okay," Boney said.

Squeak raised an eyebrow from behind his goggles. "What do you mean?"

Boney hesitated. "A clone broke into my room last night."

"What?!" Sam and Squeak exclaimed.

Boney sat in his comfy chair. "I tried to call Squeak on the Tele-tube to warn him, but he didn't answer. And then a whole bunch of clones were in my yard, so that blows our theory about clones travelling alone."

"Maybe they're starting to panic," Sam said. "They know we're on to them and they're trying to get as much done as possible before they all get caught."

"But why would they break into my house?" Boney asked.

"Maybe they remembered you from before," Squeak said.

"But why would they only break into Boney's house?" Sam wondered.

Squeak rested his chin in his hand, then his eyes lit up and he snapped his fingers. "Maybe it's the food!"

"The food?" Boney said. "What do you mean?"

"Well, you said your aunt gave the clones cookies, right?"

"Yeah . . ."

"And the newspaper said the Itchy clones were caught stealing pies and doughnuts."

"So . . . ?"

"So it must be the food they're after," Squeak said.

Boney puzzled over this for a moment. "I suppose it's possible . . . Anyway, if it wasn't for Tiger, I would have been toast. He kicked that clone's butt." He nuzzled the kitten.

"Good thing you had him with you," Sam said.

"What about your aunt?" Squeak asked. "Is she going to let you keep him?"

Boney smiled. "As it turns out, Tiger is not only an expert clone fighter, he's an amazing bug catcher, too."

"Ah." Squeak turned to Sam. "His aunt suffers from an uncontrollable phobia of insects."

"Oh. That's unfortunate." Sam tossed her hair. "It's actually quite a common fear." She was about to elaborate when they heard a noise at the foot of the tree.

Everyone froze. Henry raised his head and glared around the clubhouse.

A mop of red hair rose slowly into view. "What's for breakfast?" Itchy asked, his head popping up through Escape Hatch #1.

Squeak and Sam exhaled with relief.

Boney growled, "Get in here. You're late, as usual. And why are you wearing my Superman T-shirt? We agreed last night: full regalia!"

Itchy looked down at his shirt. "I was in a hurry and I had nothing else to wear. And how should I know what, 'full regalia' means?"

Boney gestured at Sam, who was dressed to military precision, including a military-issue camouflage vest and knapsack. "Sam knew what it meant."

"Well, goody for Sam," Itchy grunted.

Squeak raised an eyebrow. "I question the wisdom of dressing exactly like the clones we're trying to defeat."

Itchy shot him a wry look. "Thanks, Army Spock. I preferred it when you had a crush on Leonardo da Vinci."

"Who has a crush on da Vinci?" Sam asked.

Squeak spoke through clenched teeth. "He's being totally illogical. And he's evading the question."

Itchy rolled his eyes. "Well, excuse me, Your Royal Spockness, but my mom hasn't done laundry yet."

"So . . . you couldn't have worn a different dirty shirt?" Boney said, jumping up from his chair. "We won't be able to tell you apart from the rest of the clones."

"This was the least-dirty shirt I have right now. It doesn't stink." Itchy sniffed his armpit as proof.

Boney grimaced with disgust. "I could have lent you something else."

"And have you harassing me for the rest of my life? No way."

"You could learn to do your own laundry," Sam suggested. "It's not that difficult."

Squeak looked at her with surprise. "That's what I'm always telling him."

Itchy pouted. "Why don't you all just gang up on me."

"We're not ganging up on you," Boney said.

"Yes, you are!"

"I have a fun surprise." Sam swung her knapsack off her shoulder and unzipped it. Reaching in, she pulled out a handful of purple-checkered material and handed the boys a small bundle of cloth each. "There's one for everyone."

"Thanks," Squeak said, before he even knew what it was.

Itchy held the article at arm's length as though he had just dug it out from the garbage. "Uhhh . . . What is it? Underwear?"

"Field dressings?" Boney guessed.

"Kitten holders!" Sam said. "I made them last night. You wear them like a sling." She demonstrated by pulling the sling over her head and slipping Fluffy in, adjusting the cloth until the kitten was comfortably situated.

Squeak slipped the sling over his shoulder and placed his kitten inside. "Neat."

"This way we can carry our kittens and have our hands free," Sam explained.

"Cool." Boney put on his sling, tucking Tiger in.

Sam turned to Itchy. "Yours is slightly bigger to accommodate Henry."

"They're a little loud, don't you think?" Itchy complained. "They clash with your camouflage."

"It was the best I could do with the materials I had on hand."

"We may as well wave a red flag," Itchy grumbled.

"Purple," Squeak joked.

"Just put it on," Boney ordered.

Itchy put on the sling and placed Henry inside. The

rooster fluffed his feathers and nestled down, his head poking out.

"Ingenious," Squeak said.

Itchy patted Henry on the head, then pulled a cheese sandwich out of nowhere and began to eat. "So what's the plan?"

"The same as last night," Boney said. "We go back to the warehouse and scout around. If we're lucky, we'll find the Mother Ship."

Itchy bobbled his head. "If we're lucky?"

"You know what I mean. Maybe we can catch them off guard."

"Catch them off guard . . . ?" Itchy repeated. "That's your plan?"

Boney gave him an irritated look.

Itchy turned to Squeak and Sam. "Seriously? That's really your plan?"

"Do you have any better ideas?" Boney asked.

Itchy took a bite from his sandwich. "I'm just saying . . . it doesn't sound like much of a plan to me."

"It's all we've got right now."

"Fine."

Boney shot him another look and continued. "As I was saying . . . We'll follow the train tracks the way we did before. Everyone remember to stick close together — and no heroics."

Itchy smirked. "No problem there."

Boney addressed Sam. "Do you have the Disruptor and the electro-node-a-metre?"

Sam touched a little leather pouch on her belt. "Locked and loaded."

"Good," Boney said. "Then let's go."

CHAPTER SEVENTEEN

MIND CONTROL

The sun was reaching over the treetops as the band of friends moved along the train tracks to the opening at the edge of the woods. Boney gestured for the troop to wait while he left the tracks and crouched in the shade at the foot of the path, looking for clues. The sunlight glinted through the leaves; a light breeze sighed in the tree branches. Boney looked around to be sure the coast was clear, then signalled for the gang to join him.

Squeak crouched beside Boney. "Any evidence of recent activity?" He pulled his telescope from his messenger bag and scanned the woods.

Boney pointed at a clump of bushes. "Some broken branches and about a thousand more footprints since yesterday."

Sam produced the electro-node-a-metre from her knapsack and held it out in front of her, pressing the silver button. The thin wire arms rose from the sides of the device and began to whirl around, the small glass globes at the ends of the arms firing up and reflecting like Christmas lights in the lenses of Squeak's goggles. Itchy pulled a gigantic package of licorice from Henry's sling and stripped a couple of pieces from the pack.

Boney stared at him incredulously. "You're keeping your licorice in the sling next to Henry?"

"It's easier to get to." Itchy waved the licorice at Boney. "Want a piece?"

"Uh . . . no thanks."

Itchy offered the licorice to Squeak, who raised an eyebrow and shook his head. Then he reluctantly turned to Sam, who politely refused. "Suit yourself," he said, stuffing the pack back into Henry's sling.

Sam continued to scan the area, moving the electro-node-a-metre along the ground and up toward the broken branches of the bushes, the arms spinning faster and faster. "The clones have definitely been busy."

Itchy chewed on his licorice. "Doing what?"

"It's anyone's guess." Sam turned off the device and stowed it safely in her pouch. "But I suppose we'll find out soon enough."

"It's unusually quiet in the woods today," Squeak observed. "I can't hear any birds at all — or the humming."

"What humming?" Itchy asked.

"The humming from the warehouse," Boney said.

"The clones hum?" Itchy pulled another piece of licorice from the pack, gobbling it down.

"Not the clones, the warehouse," Boney said.

Itchy swallowed. "The warehouse hums?"

"Not the warehouse, per se. The machine that makes the clones, I think."

"But the clones themselves don't hum?"

"They might hum. How should I know?" Boney said.

Itchy shrugged. "You seem to know everything else."

Boney frowned. "What is wrong with you?"

"What?"

"This isn't a joke, you know."

"Do you see me laughing?"

"Gentlemen, please," Squeak intervened.

Itchy and Boney turned to see Sam staring at them in disbelief. Itchy folded his arms self-consciously. Boney straightened his sling, Tiger purring inside. "Shall we continue?" Boney said.

The four friends skulked along the path, Itchy obsessively munching on licorice and practically walking on Squeak's heels as Boney continued to point out indicators that the clones had been on the move.

"We should reach the warehouse any minute," he said. "It should be just around this bend in the path."

Boney walked ahead about fifty feet, and then back-tracked. "It should be here," he insisted. He turned around where he stood. "I can't believe this. It's gone."

"Are you sure we're in the right place?" Squeak asked.

"I'm positive!"

Squeak retrieved his telescope and searched the woods. "This is highly irregular."

Itchy chewed on his licorice, looking hopeful. "Maybe the clones packed up their tent and left."

"How could they just leave?" Boney said, pacing back and forth. "There was a giant warehouse here yesterday, with blue lights and a huge machine inside, and hundreds, maybe thousands, of clones!"

Itchy waved a piece of licorice at the empty spot. "Well, they're not here now."

"It does appear that the clones have left," Squeak said. "The kittens aren't at all alarmed—and neither is Henry." The rooster snored in Itchy's sling. "If the clones were here, wouldn't our animal companions be concerned?"

"We don't know how close we have to be to the clones before Henry and the kittens will respond to their presence," Sam said. "We've only ever seen their response at close range. Besides, the electro-node-a-metre gave a strong positive reading that the clones are in the area."

She pulled a pair of binoculars from her bag and began searching the site.

Squeak scoured the forest with his telescope.

"No movement of any kind on the west end," Sam reported.

"The east side is also clear," Squeak said.

Boney pulled on his chin. "Maybe they relocated the warehouse to avoid further detection. Let's try moving deeper into the woods." He motioned for the group to fall out, causing Sam and Squeak to turn abruptly, Squeak's telescope hitting Sam's binoculars and nearly knocking them from her hands.

His face turned instantly red. "Oh, sorry." He clapped his telescope shut and placed it back in his bag.

Sam also blushed, fumbling with her binoculars as she placed them in her knapsack.

Seconds later, Henry woke with a start. He made a low clucking noise. This roused the kittens, who instantly growled as they trained their eyes on a point deep in the woods.

"Clone alert!" Boney whispered.

Itchy jumped behind him, peering over his shoulder. "I can't see anything."

"Over there! Ten o'clock!" Squeak pointed to a spot in the trees.

"I see them," Sam said. "They seem to be on the move. Let's go."

"Do we have to?" Itchy whined, but Boney, Squeak, and Sam were already creeping through the trees. He groaned. "This can't be a good idea."

Boney pressed his finger to his lips. "Shhh . . . If they hear you, we're in big trouble."

Itchy imitated him, pressing his finger to his lips to show he understood. Then he crossed his heart and stuffed another piece of licorice into his mouth.

The friends crept forward, huddling in a tight group. They stopped behind a clump of bushes, watching. The kittens flattened their ears and hissed. Henry clucked low in his gizzard.

The clones moved single file through the forest, faces vacant, small meeping sounds emanating from their lips. Their feet seemed made of lead as they lumbered like sleepwalkers, their arms outstretched.

"There must be millions of them," Itchy said. "And every one looks exactly like me!" He stepped on a twig, the sharp snap echoing through the forest. The four friends froze with fear as several clones whipped their heads around to discover the source of the sound, their empty eyes searching the woods. But they soon forgot what they were looking for and turned away, urged on by some invisible signal that seemed to control them.

"What's wrong with them?" Itchy asked. "Where are they going and why are they all moving like that?"

"Hive mentality—like ants," Squeak explained. "They're likely being organized through some kind of electromagnetic impulse."

"Mind control," Sam said. "We were right."

Squeak nodded. "It's quite effective on less intelligent life forms."

Itchy scoffed with amusement. "Stupid clones . . . thinking they can impersonate me . . ."

"What are they carrying?" Boney asked.

Sam studied the clones through her binoculars. "It's food. They're all carrying food."

Itchy's nose twitched. "Food?"

"So our theory was correct," Squeak said. "The clones must have attacked Boney's house in search of things to eat."

"But why do they need all this food?" Boney wondered.

Itchy licked his lips. "What kind of food?"

"Sweets." Sam adjusted the focus on her binoculars. "Doughnuts, cakes, chocolate, cream puffs, jars of caramel sauce . . . whole bags of sugar."

Itchy drooled. "Really? Where are they going with all that amazing stuff?"

"That's what we're here to find out," Boney said. He signalled to Sam and Squeak to move to the right and flank the clones. "Stay hidden. And under no circumstances should you engage the enemy. We just want to determine where they're going at this point. Understood?"

Squeak and Sam saluted. Boney saluted back. He turned to speak to Itchy but found Henry instead, staring at him with his yellow eyes, his purple sling abandoned on the ground. Boney picked up the sling in shock. "Itchy's gone!"

CHAPTER EIGHTEEN

THE MOTHER SHIP

Itchy moved through the woods as though hypno-tized, his arms held out in front of him, his hands clutching the half-eaten package of red licorice.

"Itchy, NO!" Boney cried. He made to run, but Sam grabbed his shirt.

"It's too dangerous."

Boney pulled away from Sam's grasp. "But we have to help him! His mind is being controlled!"

"We can't just rush in," Sam said. "If we alert the clones, then we'll all be in trouble. We'll follow him until we have a chance to get him back without attract-ing any attention."

"That would be the best plan," Squeak agreed.

Boney ran his hand through his hair. "But what if they discover he's not one of them?"

"I don't think that should be a problem," Squeak said.

The three friends watched as Itchy plodded toward the clones and took his place at the back of the line. Henry clucked and fussed. The kittens growled. Itchy moved in rhythm with the rest of the clones, small meeping noises bubbling from his lips.

All at once, a whistle screeched, shattering the silence. Boney, Sam, and Squeak covered their ears, buckling in agony. Henry squawked in alarm while the kittens mewed with terror. Itchy and the clones turned their pale faces upward in one synchronized sweep, staring at something only they could see. After several excruciating seconds, the whistle stopped. The line of clones lurched forward as they began to march, their feet stomping on the forest floor, their motions exaggerated and rigid.

Boney lowered his hands from his ears. "What was that?"

"Some sort of signal." Sam cleared her ears with her fingers, then checked to make sure Fluffy was okay.

Boney pulled Itchy's sling over his other shoulder and placed Henry inside, positioning the two slings so they wouldn't interfere with each other. "Let's go," he said. "And stay frosty. We can't afford any mistakes." He rushed off, Squeak and Sam following behind.

The three friends trailed Itchy and the rest of the clones, careful not to be seen. The kittens hissed, while Henry clucked angrily.

Squeak noted a group of clones that seemed to appear from nowhere in the woods. "There are more joining the procession."

The clones took their position in line, marching mechanically. Sam jerked to a stop, grabbing Boney and Squeak by the sleeves. She pointed to a spot in the woods ahead.

"I don't see anything," Boney whispered.

Sam continued to point. "See how the clones seem to just disappear . . ."

Boney squinted through the filtered light of the forest. Then he nodded. "Yeah, I see what you mean. The clones are fading into nothing."

"Not fading," Squeak corrected him. "They must be stepping into something we can't see — probably hidden by some sort of cloaking device."

Boney looked at him with confusion.

"The Mother Ship," Squeak said.

The clones continued to vanish, one by one, until Itchy was third in line.

Boney clenched his jaw. "We have to stop him before he disappears."

But it was too late. Itchy marched forward, vanishing into thin air. The remaining clones followed, until the three friends were alone in the woods.

"Come on," Sam said. "We have to move or we may

lose him forever." She raced toward the spot where Itchy had seemed to vapourize.

Boney streaked after her, Henry and Tiger bouncing in their slings. "Man, she's fast."

"Wait for me!" Squeak ran behind him, holding his sling with one hand like a football to prevent Spock from flying out.

Sam skidded on her feet, turned and waved Boney and Squeak on, hesitated, then stepped forward and vanished. Boney ran faster, but, in his haste, he caught his combat boot on a log and tripped. Flying through the air with a yelp, he somehow managed to twist mid-flight so as not to crush Tiger and Henry when he fell. The rooster squawked resentfully as they hit the ground. Tiger yowled with fright. Without missing a beat, Boney jumped to his feet with a grunt, just in time to see Squeak scuttle to a stop at the exact point in the woods where Sam had hesitated.

"Look!" Squeak said, retrieving Sam's electro-node-a-metre from the ground. "She must have dropped it."

Boney ran up and stumbled into him, sending Squeak crashing forward to disappear without a trace. "Whoa." Boney stared at the spot of ground where Squeak had stood. The trail of footprints ended there. Henry and Tiger looked at him with serious faces, as though they understood the situation. Boney straightened himself.

"I guess it's now or never." He took a deep breath and stepped forward.

A strange buzzing sound filled his ears. The air pressed around him. He seemed to be passing through a mild electrical field that pulsed in waves through his body. The air felt thick and magnetized. Boney shouldered against the force, leaning heavily, until he popped out the other side. Staggering to regain his balance, he found Squeak blinking angrily up at him from a heap on the floor of the craft.

"You pushed me," Squeak said, his voice strangely muffled and high-pitched.

"I didn't mean to." Boney's hand flew to his throat when he heard the ridiculous pitch of his own voice. "Wow, this is totally freaky. We sound like Alvin and the Chipmunks."

Tiger mewed a high-pitched little mew.

"Even the kitten is affected," Boney said. "I hope this doesn't hurt him."

Squeak shook his head. "It's okay. It's just helium, I think. They must pipe it into the air to prevent the clones from getting the bends when they board the ship."

Boney held his hand out to help Squeak up. "What's 'the bends'?"

"Decompression sickness." Squeak stood and adjusted his goggles. "It happens when you move from an area of high pressure to an area of lower pressure, like when a scuba diver rises to the surface of the water too quickly. The aliens must live in an environment with less gravity than ours, therefore requiring some kind of transitional chamber for non-alien visitors."

Boney thought about this. "Non-alien visitors? As in, humans?"

"Or clones of humans," Squeak said.

Boney looked around the chamber. They were standing on some kind of silver gangplank. The air was a strange blue colour, like the light they'd seen glowing through the warehouse windows. There was a tunnel of some kind at the top of the gangplank, with an eerie white mist swirling around inside. Rows of little lights ran along the length of the tunnel so that it looked like an airstrip illuminated in the fog. Boney shivered. "It's cold in here."

Squeak examined the wall of the ship. It appeared to be sweating, despite the cold temperature. "Helium conducts heat away from the body."

Boney rubbed his arms to bring the warmth back to them. "Will we sound like the Chipmunks forever?"

"It's temporary," Squeak assured him. He gave Spock a scratch under the chin, then continued to inspect the wall. "I'd like to get a sample of this."

"Where's Sam?" Boney asked.

"She must have gone ahead." Squeak ran his finger down the wall, and then lightly tasted the liquid on his fingertips.

"We should get going, too." Boney walked to the top of the gangplank. He stopped and stared into the tunnel, listening to the muffled peeps and blips swirling around in the mist. As he stood there, he began feeling light in the head. He poked delicately at the mist with his finger. "What do you think it is?"

Squeak walked up the gangplank and studied the fog in the tunnel. "I guess we'll find out soon enough."

Boney pushed his hand into the mist. "It feels okay."

"It's probably another transitional zone to help us acclimatize to the alien atmosphere," Squeak said. "I'm sure it's safe."

The two boys looked at each other.

Boney swallowed. "Well . . . here goes . . ."

The boys stepped simultaneously into the tunnel.

"Hey, it's kind of neat in here," Squeak giggled.

Boney waved his arms up and down, making swirling patterns in the mist. The kittens chirped contentedly while Henry swayed happily back and forth in his sling. Boney looked at Squeak in surprise. "What is this stuff?"

Squeak twirled around, smiling. "I believe it's nitrous oxide."

"Nitrous what?"

"Ox-ide," Squeak answered, emphasizing the syllables. "Otherwise known as EN-TWO-OH. Otherwise known as *laughing gas*." He snorted and doubled over. "It enhances suggestibility and . . . and i-ma-gi-NA-tion."

Boney pointed at him. "Hey, look at Mr. Spock, being all hilarious." He started laughing like it was the funniest thing he'd ever seen. Then he stopped and became serious. "Do you think the . . . 'space people'" — he made exaggerated quotation marks with his fingers — "are trying to control our minds?"

Squeak stared at him soberly, then gave a huge, gap-toothed grin. "Naaah. Nitrous oxide is a natural . . . uhhh . . . *component* of the earth's atmosphere." He traced a big circle in the air with his hands. "This must be where the 'space people'" — he mimicked Boney's exaggerated quotation marks — "generate the atmosphere for the ship." He cackled and jumped, kicking his feet in the air. "Look! I'm as light as a feather!" He floated several yards along the tunnel before touching down. "The gravity is really light in here."

Boney's eyes bulged with astonishment, and then he took a huge leap, turning a somersault before landing on his feet.

Squeak laughed hysterically. "*That* was really cool."

"Yeah? Watch this!" Boney scuttled his feet, walking right up the side of the tunnel, flipping over, and scurrying down the other side.

The two boys giggled as they grabbed hands, waltzing together through the mist. They twirled each other around before stumbling out into a strange white vestibule. They stood, hand in hand, until their giddiness slowly lifted and they jumped away from each other with embarrassment.

"That was weird," Boney said in a normal voice. "Hey! I have my voice back!"

"I told you it was temporary." Squeak looked around the room.

The vestibule was some kind of hub, with a dozen identical corridors radiating from its centre. The entire room was seamless, like a giant mushroom, and blindingly white.

"Everything looks the same," Boney said. "How are we supposed to know which way to go?"

Squeak reached into his bag and held up Sam's electro-node-a-metre. "With this." He depressed the button on the device. The arms rose and the little glass globes began to whirl and glow. Squeak slowly turned where he stood, testing the corridors for recent activity. The arms of the electro-node-a-metre whirled fast, then slow, alternating according to their position. Squeak swept the unit back and forth several times. "This middle corridor seems to elicit the strongest response — if I'm reading the metre correctly."

Boney shrugged. "It's the best we've got. Come on."

The two boys advanced along the corridor, eyes as big as searchlights. From time to time little bursts of mist puffed from small portals in the walls and ceiling, causing the boys to jump in alarm.

"This ship must be huge," Boney said.

Squeak held his finger to his lips and nodded toward Spock. The kitten's ears were flat; he growled deep in his chest. Tiger and Henry were also on red alert, their eyes wide and searching.

"We must be close," Squeak whispered. He tilted his head, listening. "Do you hear that low thumping?"

Boney strained his ears. "Yeah, I can hear it. What do you think it is?"

Squeak pushed on the bridge of his goggles. "It sounds somewhat mechanical. Like a pump motor of some kind. I wonder where it's coming from."

"Over there!" Boney pointed down the corridor to a pool of green light wavering over the floor.

CHAPTER NINETEEN

A GHASTLY SIGHT

Boney and Squeak slunk along the corridor toward the green light, the thumping sound growing louder with every step. Crouching low, they approached an opening in the wall, Henry and the kittens growling warnings that the clones were near. As they drew closer to the light, Boney put his hand over his nose in disgust.

"What's that wretched stench?"

Squeak winced, pinching his nose. "Ugh! It smells like rotten eggs." He pulled two camouflage bandanas from his messenger bag and handed one to Boney, tying the other over his nose and mouth like a bandit from the Old West.

Boney quickly did the same, choking on the disgusting smell.

When they reached the edge of the doorway, Boney prodded the green light with his finger to be sure it was safe before he and Squeak peeked around the corner into the room. The two friends stared in horror as their eyes adjusted to the nauseating green light.

At the centre of the room sat a gigantic, blubbery blob of a creature, the size of a small school bus, reclining on a giant, round white cushion. Its skin was green and slimy, and its toothless mouth was so big it eclipsed the creature's entire body as it flapped open and shut. It had bulging yellow eyes like a bullfrog, and it slobbered and burped and gurgled and farted as it ate, filling the room with a putrid green gas.

To one side of the creature was a two-storey chute firing cannonballs of candy and cakes and sweets into the blob's gaping maw. The chute was fed by the Itchy clones, shuffling in a long line, waiting to climb the metal stairs that led to the opening of the machine to dump their cargo. Once deposited, the sweets were shot from the chute with a loud *bang*, the clones making their way across a catwalk and down another set of stairs to gather in a loose group on the other side of the room.

The boys cringed as the cannon suddenly misfired, overshooting the blob and splattering the food against the wall in a revolting smear of blue icing and whipped cream. This caused the creature to scream with rage and pound the floor with its tail, knocking several terrified clones off the catwalk to be gobbled up as they tumbled into the creature's flapping mouth. The blob shuddered as it swallowed the clones. It convulsed and grew in size.

Boney stared at Squeak. "Did that blob thing just get bigger?"

Squeak raised his eyebrows. "It appears to have grown after eating the clones."

"Who's that over there?" Boney pointed to a shadowy figure crouched behind a low white wall near the front of the room.

The figure seemed to hear him, because it turned, the features of its ghoulish face wavering in the noxious green light. Its eyes were big and round, and it had a long trunk stretching down where its nose and mouth should have been.

The boys gasped, ducking out of sight.

"It's an alien!" Boney said, trying to remain calm. "I think it saw us!"

After several moments when nothing happened, the boys peeped around the corner again. The alien was still staring at them. Only this time, it gestured for them to come forward.

Squeak strained to see through the green atmosphere in the room. "Ummm . . . that's not an alien. It's Sam, wearing a gas mask."

Boney rubbed his eyes. "Are you sure? It's hard to see anything through this disgusting air."

Henry blinked against the fumes. The kittens rubbed their eyes with their paws.

"How'd Sam get in there without being seen?" Boney wondered.

"She must have waited until there was a distraction," Squeak guessed.

"Good thinking. The next time that blob freaks out, we'll dash behind that wall and join her."

No sooner did Boney say this than the cannon misfired, blasting a huge lump of chocolate éclairs over the blob's head. The éclairs exploded against the wall, sending the creature into a fit of pounding and screeching. It knocked more clones off the catwalk and into its voracious jaws.

"Now!" Boney said, as the blob shuddered and increased in size. He grabbed Squeak by the sleeve and dragged him into the room, skidding to a stop beside Sam.

"What took you so long?" Sam's voice sounded tinny and clipped through the voicemitter on her gas mask.

"We thought you were one of them," Boney said. "Where did you get that gas mask?"

Sam's voicemitter clicked. "I keep it in my military knapsack at all times, just in case."

The three friends turned to watch as the blob continued to eat, its giant mouth blubbering and slobbering, big clouds of green gas filling the air.

"What *is* that disgusting thing?" Boney asked.

Sam shook her head. "Some kind of intergalactic glutton that requires massive amounts of sugar to sustain itself. It's obviously dangerous, judging by the height of that chute and the way it keeps eating the clones."

There was a loud rasping sound, like someone pinching the air out of a balloon, and the blob released another giant plume of gas.

Boney grimaced. "Why doesn't it stay on its own planet and eat? Why does it have to come here and eat all our cakes and stuff?"

The blob belched, causing Boney and Squeak to cover their noses with disgust.

"It likely consumed its entire planet and needed a new source of sugar." Squeak choked against the fumes.

Boney gagged. "It's giving me the dry heaves."

Squeak scoped the room. "Where's Itchy?"

Sam pointed to a figure near the end of the clone line.

"How can you tell it's him?" Boney coughed. "They all look identical."

Sam handed her binoculars to Boney. "He's carrying red licorice. And look at his neck. There's no mark. The clones have small puncture marks on the backs of their necks, as though they've been inflated by some kind of needle — like a football."

Boney held the binoculars to his burning eyes and

studied the hordes of clones as best he could. "Okay, I see him. But that puncture mark on the clones will be difficult to use as a form of detection. It's just too small. The minute Itchy drops that licorice into the chute, he'll join that big group and we'll never be able to tell him apart from the clones." He handed the binoculars back to Sam. "We have to get him out of here now."

There was a sudden loud clunk and a series of panels on the ceiling slid open, revealing dozens of large grey fans. They powered up, whirling faster and faster until the entire ship seemed to vibrate. The fans drew the noxious green gas from the room, the gas whirling in huge funnel clouds toward the ceiling.

"Thank heavens," Boney said, letting go of his nose as the fans cleared the air.

Sam removed her gas mask and stuffed it into her bag. She investigated the fans through her binoculars. "I wonder what that's all about?"

Squeak produced his telescope. "They seem to be collecting the gas."

"What for?" Boney asked.

"I don't know. But we'd better figure it out soon," Squeak said. "Itchy's nearly reached the mouth of the chute."

Itchy staggered up the last few steps on the stairs. He clomped in a trance across the catwalk, holding his package of red licorice in front of him. When he reached the opening of the chute, he stopped. The other clones began to bottleneck behind him, bumping against each other.

"What's he doing?" Boney hissed.

Squeak pushed on the bridge of his goggles. "He's probably having second thoughts about giving the blob his licorice. He's fighting the mind control because he wants to keep the candy for himself. You know he's always had difficulty sharing."

"He's going to have some serious difficulty if he doesn't move soon."

The clones on the stairs looked around in confusion. The blob started slobbering violently when the cannonballs of food stopped coming.

Boney groaned. "Drop the licorice in the chute, Itchy."

But Itchy just stood there, motionless. Until an alarm sounded, blaring through the room. Lights started to flash, and the blob began to screech and roar, banging its tail on the floor. The clones panicked, breaking ranks and moving erratically through the room. The alarm continued to blast as a row of small doors along the periphery of the room whooshed open and dozens of small grey aliens came rushing out. They were wearing blue overalls and what appeared to be silver rubber boots. Their heads were pointed, and their huge black eyes were slanted upward. And they looked very upset.

"Third-level Greys!" Sam exclaimed.

"What are third-level Greys?" Boney asked.

"Drones," she said. "They must be the ones harvesting the noxious gases from the blob. They were alerted by that alarm."

Boney clenched his jaw. "We're really in a mess now."

CHAPTER TWENTY

BATTLE OF THE CLONES

The alarm continued to sound as the little grey men in blue overalls scattered throughout the room. A group of them scuttled over to where the blob sat, carrying silver buckets and long spoons of some sort. They began waving and jumping in front of the creature's enraged face, and then they attempted to appease the beast by flinging huge spoonfuls of goop from the buckets into its mouth. But their aim was terrible and they kept missing, launching gobs of glop over the beast's head or misfiring completely and sending the goop onto the floor at their feet. This served to infuriate the creature further, and it began howling and pounding more feverishly than before. The little men tried to dodge the creature's tail, but they were knocked off their feet and gobbled up along with their goop buckets and spoons. Another group of little grey men rushed to take their place, carrying more buckets of glop and even longer spoons, only to slip on the goopy floor and succumb to the same fate as their alien colleagues.

"How horrible," Sam groaned, clutching her stomach.

Boney winced. "What a way to go . . ."

"They're obviously expendable," Squeak said.

The entire time this was going on, the rest of the little grey men were trying to wrangle the disoriented clones, herding them like frightened turkeys into groups against the wall. Several of the workers stormed the stairs to unblock the clog that Itchy and his licorice had caused.

"We have to get Itchy out of there," Boney said. "Somebody, do something!"

Sam pulled the Disruptor from her bag and depressed the switch. A huge wave exploded from the device, radiating like a nuclear blast through the room. It hit the clones and the little grey men and the blob sitting on its seat. Instantly, the clones became zombies, wandering and meeping and bumping into each other. The little grey men seemed perplexed as they watched the clones, trying to figure out what had just happened. The blob yawned a huge slimy yawn and blinked its bulging yellow eyes at a mystified group of grey men who stood beneath the flashing lights of the alarm, still holding their buckets and spoons at the ready. Itchy swayed on the catwalk in front of the chute, his knees buckling slightly.

"It worked," Boney softly cheered. He was just about to congratulate Sam when Itchy jerked with a kind of spasm and dropped the package of licorice into the chute. There was a loud clunk, and the machine spewed black smoke as it belched out the licorice, package and all, right into the face of the blob. Yowling with surprise, the creature began pounding and screaming once again. The clones came back to life and started marching maniacally around the room, the little grey men desperately trying to control them. The group of workers on the stairs rushed toward Itchy.

"Push the Disruptor button again!" Boney yelled.

Sam pushed the button, sending another wave through the room. But this time it did nothing, bouncing harmlessly off the walls. Sam looked helplessly at Boney and Squeak. "I guess it doesn't have the same effect twice in a row."

Boney grabbed the device and began frantically pushing the button over and over. Squeak pried the Disruptor from Boney's hands. "It won't work!"

Boney jumped to his feet. "Well, I'm not going to just stand here and watch Itchy get eaten by that creature!" He rushed toward the stairs that led up to the chute.

"Oh dear . . ." Squeak moaned. "This is awful."

Boney launched himself up the stairs, pushing and shoving past the befuddled clones. As he ran, Henry and Tiger squawked and hissed in their slings, pecking and scratching any clones that got too close. Some of the clones were so surprised by the attack that they simply flipped like manikins over the railing, landing in a heap on the floor. Across the room, little grey men stood in shock, chattering and pointing at the spectacle being played out before them.

Boney reached the top of the stairs and grabbed Itchy, who began shouting in terror, his eyes empty and lifeless.

"Itchy, it's me!" Boney yelled in his face.

But Itchy just kept hollering like a startled sleepwalker. Boney shook his friend with all his might. Itchy howled back like a madman, his head bobbling around on his neck like a dust mop. When he wouldn't stop shouting, Boney raised his hand and slapped Itchy sharply across the face.

"Ow!" Itchy yelped. He rubbed his cheek with his hand. "What'd you hit me for?"

Boney placed the sling holding Henry over Itchy's shoulders. "We have to get out of here. The clones are going to get us."

"Clones!" Itchy started hollering all over again.

Boney grabbed his arm and dragged him down the stairs. "Come on!"

General mayhem ensued as clones marched, the blob screeched, and workers scampered around, unsure of what to do. This helped Boney and Itchy to escape undetected, and they were almost at the bottom of the stairs when one of the little grey men came to his senses. Extending his skinny grey finger, he pressed a button on the wall of the ship.

A whistle shrilled, jerking the clones to attention. Their heads turned, hundreds of vacant eyes trained on Boney and Itchy. The boys stood, petrified.

"The clones are going to attack!" Sam cried.

The clones mobilized, converging on the two boys from the top and bottom of the stairs.

"What are we going to do?" Itchy wailed.

"Jump!" Boney said.

The two boys scissored over the railing and landed with a thump on the floor, a wall of angry clones staring back at them. The clones took a unified step forward. Boney and Itchy stepped back. Henry raised his comb, ruffling his feathers in warning. Tiger puffed up his fur and hissed, his ears pressed flat against his head.

Sam turned to Squeak. "We have to help them." She sprang from behind the wall to stand beside Boney and Itchy.

"Wait for me!" Squeak called, running after her.

The four friends formed a circle, standing back to back for greater protection.

"This could be the end," Boney said over his shoulder. "It's been nice knowing you."

Itchy's bottom lip began to quiver. "Please don't say that. There's so much food I want to eat."

"I'll never complain about my aunt's cooking again," Boney vowed.

"What will my dad do without me?" Squeak whistled through the gap in his teeth.

Itchy moaned. "I'm only twelve. I'm too young to die!"

"We're not going to die," Sam said. "We have to stay positive."

"Oh, sure," Itchy blubbered. "That's easy for you to say."

The clones growled, surging forward. The Odds raised their fists, Itchy's knobby knees knocking together.

Sam assumed a ninja pose. "We're not going down without a fight!" She rushed the clones, leaping through the air. With one swift kick, she flattened three clones, karate-chopping two more to the floor before her feet even hit the ground. Fluffy jumped from his sling and landed on the floundering clones, spitting and scratching until their faces were covered in welts. The clones staggered to their feet, blind and stumbling, until they crashed together, collapsing in a heap like the poles of a cheap tent. The little grey men dissolved into a confused panic, running around the room clutching their heads as Sam felled clones with her lethal kicks.

"Wow!" Squeak said. "She's totally awesome!"

But despite Sam's efforts, the clones kept coming. With each one defeated, five more took its place. In a flurry of punches and roundhouse kicks, Sam scattered them like bowling pins. Fluffy finished them off, levelling clones in a blur of flying claws.

"Come on!" Boney yelled. "Sam needs us!"

"She seems to be doing fine by herself," Itchy quavered.

Squeak bolted forward, doubling over and hollering at the top of his lungs. He rushed the clones, driving one in the stomach with his head, like a battering ram. The clone reeled back, hitting the clones behind it, so that they fell in a row like dominoes, right into the blob's slimy mouth. The creature greedily gobbled them up and convulsed as it swelled several times in size before releasing a floor-shaking burp.

A group of grey men began waving frenetically, attempting to direct the clones away from the blob. But the clones crashed through them, knocking little grey men into the blob's ravenous mouth. Boney shouted encouragement. "Keep going, Squeak! You're taking them out like flies!"

Boney rushed into the fray, punching and shoving the clones into the mouth of the beast. Itchy stood where he was, his pale fists shaking in the air. A clone trained its eyes on him and advanced, growling and gnashing.

"Get away from me!" Itchy shrieked, slapping hysterically at the clone.

The clone slapped back, until both of them were shrieking and slapping like maniacs. Henry leaped from his sling and attacked, his rooster spurs slicing the air, his wings beating the clone about the head as he pecked at its eyes. The clone covered its face, lurching backward. Boney shoved it toward the blob, which slobbered it down with a loud smack.

The four friends fought like Spartans, their kittens scratching and snarling along with them, Henry flapping and pecking at Itchy's side. They threw more and more clones at the blob, the creature's big yellow eyes nearly popping from its head as it swallowed and convulsed and expanded. The room reeked with green gas, the creature farting and burping and gurgling.

Then all at once there was a deafening explosion, like the sound of a Zeppelin hitting a blowtorch. The room shook as steaming green guck flew through the air and a giant mushroom cloud of foul gas roiled to the ceiling. Green goo splattered everywhere, sliming the walls and clones and little grey men. It showered down on the kittens and the rooster and on the four friends, who gaped at each other in shock.

"The blob blew up!" Boney shouted, choking on the acrid gas.

Sam, Squeak, and Itchy coughed and sputtered, gasping for air. Squeak used his fingers to squeegee the slime from his goggles so he could get a better look at the carnage.

In the middle of the room, where the blob once sat, was a smoking pile of green slime. The clones shuffled through the sludge, coughing and meeping, while the little grey men wrung their hands. Squeak poked the heap of steaming goop with the toe of his combat boot. "I've never seen anything like it before."

"Neither have I," Sam said. She pulled a tongue depressor and a small plastic bottle from her bag and took a sample of the sludge, the green slime jiggling like rancid Jell-O.

Itchy flinched. "That's disgusting." But his face lit up as he licked the slime from his lips. "Hey! This green glop tastes pretty good. It's really sweet."

Boney winced. "Now *that* is truly disgusting."

Henry shook his feathers. The kittens preened the goop from their fur. From somewhere in the room the whistle sounded again, followed by a stream of weird clicks and bleeps. The fans in the ceiling whirred to life, sucking the gas into the vents. A door mysteriously opened in the wall and the clones began marching in a line from the room. Another door appeared, and the little grey men scurried away, leaving the four friends standing alone in a sea of steaming goop. The doors zipped shut and there was an eerie silence.

CHAPTER TWENTY-ONE

DOUBLE TROUBLE

Boney looked around the room. "What's happening now?"

"Who cares?" Itchy said. "I'm not standing around to find out. Let's get out of here." He grabbed Henry, stuffed him into the sling, and bolted toward the door, his skinny legs flailing.

"Itchy, wait!" Boney called after him. "You have no idea where you're going." He picked up Tiger and placed him in his sling before chasing after his friend.

Squeak and Sam picked up their kittens and did the same. They skidded through the green slime as they shot out the door, only to find Boney and Itchy staring, bewildered, down the corridor.

"Do you remember which way we came?" Boney asked.

"Veer left," Sam said.

The four friends veered left and ran down the corridor until they reached a fork in the hallway.

Boney growled in frustration. "Now what?"

Squeak produced the electro-node-a-metre and handed it to Sam.

"Hey, where'd you find it?" Sam said.

Squeak smiled. "You dropped it on your way into the ship."

Sam threw her arms around Squeak, who instantly blushed.

Boney stepped between them. "I hate to interrupt, but could we hurry, please?"

Sam flipped the switch on the wandlike device. The arms rose and began slowly turning, the little lights glowing.

"We don't have time for this," Itchy moaned.

"It'll only take a second," Sam promised, staring at the lights. "Go left," she finally said.

Itchy dashed to the left and ran smack into Boney and Squeak.

"Hey! How'd you get in front of me?" he said.

But then Boney and Squeak came running around the corner and slammed right into Itchy. Itchy stood, his head cranking back and forth between the two sets of identical friends—one in camouflage, the other in the same T-shirts and jeans the boys were wearing the day of the test flight at Starky Hill. Itchy stepped back in shock. "Tell me I'm having a nightmare."

Boney did a double-take. "What the heck is this?"

The four friends stared in awe at this new set of clones. The clones walked toward Boney and Squeak, until the two boys appeared to be looking in the mirror. The kittens hissed as the clones gazed at the Odds with the disaffected curiosity of a velociraptor.

Sam whipped a magnifying glass from her knapsack and began examining the clones. "Just as I suspected. The aliens are raising the stakes. These clones seem more advanced than the Itchys."

Itchy scratched his bramble-bush hair. "What do you mean 'more advanced'?"

"They likely have rudimentary speech capability," Sam explained. "Nothing too complex. Probably more like a tape recorder than anything else."

"Fascinating," Squeak said.

"Fascinating," his clone repeated in the exact same manner.

"He sounds just like you!" Boney exclaimed.

"He sounds just like you!" Boney's clone said.

Sam peered into the clone's ear. "I imagine they're building a database of sound bites by repeating your words so they can interact more successfully with real people."

Squeak frowned thoughtfully. "Do you think they simply parrot everything we say, or will they be capable of independent thought eventually?"

His clone frowned, repeating the question identically.

"I don't know," Sam said.

Squeak adjusted his goggles. His clone did the same.

"Do you think we're in any danger?" Squeak asked.

"Do you think we're in any danger?" his clone said.

Sam sniffed the clone's skin. "I don't think so . . . as long as we don't do anything stupid . . ."

"What's the square root of five million and six?" Squeak suddenly asked his clone.

"What's the square root of five million and six?" the clone asked back.

Itchy smacked himself on the forehead. "That's all we need—two of you guys."

"This is really creepy," Boney said.

"This is really creepy," his clone repeated.

"Actually, it's incredibly annoying," Boney said.

"Actually, it's incredibly annoying," his clone repeated.

"Hey, stop that," Boney snapped.

"Hey, stop that," the clone snapped back.

"Stop repeating what I say," Boney demanded.

"Stop repeating what I say," the clone demanded back.

Boney gritted his teeth. "I don't like people copying me."

"I don't like people copying me," the clone said.

Boney stuck his tongue out. The clone retaliated.

"You're a stupid meathead!" Boney snarled.

"You're a stupid meathead!" the clone snarled back.

"I know you are, but what am I?" Boney taunted.

"I know you are, but what am I?" the clone taunted back.

"Cut it out, you stupid clone!" Boney shoved the clone in the shoulder.

The clone shoved back, copying his words and actions exactly. Boney raised his fist and the clone raised its fist, too. They were about to punch each other when an entire platoon of Boneys and Squeaks appeared around the corner.

"Now we're really in trouble," Itchy wailed. He turned as though to run, but Sam stopped him.

"Wait," she said. "We don't have to fight. We can use this to our advantage."

"How?" Boney and Squeak asked together.

"How?" all their clones repeated.

"Would you please stop that?" Itchy pleaded.

The Squeaks and Boneys stared at him scornfully.

Itchy shook his head. "This is insane. What is the

purpose of replicating clones that just act exactly like the people they're cloned from?"

"I can think of several applications," Squeak said, his clones repeating his words.

"So can I," Sam agreed.

"Now everybody is repeating everyone else," Itchy groaned.

"It's not a bad thing," Sam said. "The clones simply reflect the behaviour of their originators in order to fit in. So . . . why not be kind?"

"What do you mean?" Boney asked.

"What do you mean?" his clones repeated.

"Give your clone a hug," Sam said.

"What?"

Boney's clones mimicked his surprise.

"Just do it," Sam said.

Boney stared unsympathetically at the clone in front of him. All the Boney clones stared back.

Sam nudged Boney in the ribs. "Go on."

Boney pursed his lips. His clones did the same. He hesitated, then stiffly raised his arms. The clones raised their arms together as though performing a strange ballet. Boney twisted his face like he was swallowing a bitter pill, and then put his arms around the clone and gave it a quick hug. The Boney clones twisted their faces and made a hugging motion with their arms.

"That wasn't so bad, was it?" Sam said.

Boney shrugged, his clones shrugging together in front of him.

"This is so weird," Itchy said.

"Now hug each other," Sam told Boney and Squeak.

The Squeaks looked uneasily at the Boneys.

"I've spent a whole lifetime learning to hide my feelings," Squeak said, his clones repeating his words.

"This is no time to be Spock," Itchy blustered. "Just give Boney a hug."

The Squeaks faced the Boneys. They stared at each other for a few moments, and then hugged, stepping quickly away from each other.

"Do it again," Sam directed. "But this time put some feeling into it."

The Squeaks put their arms around the Boneys and squeezed, hugging as though they hadn't seen each other in years.

"Good, good," Sam encouraged. "Now tell him you love him."

The Squeaks looked at Sam with mild concern showing through their goggles.

"It's okay," she said. "We're making really good progress here."

Squeak cleared his throat. "I love you," he mumbled.

"I love you," his clones softly chanted.

The clones kept hugging on their own, even as Boney and Squeak pulled away.

Itchy sniffed, holding back a tear. "This is so beautiful."

Sam tugged on his sleeve. She pointed down the passageway to the right. The four friends slowly tiptoed away, leaving the clones hugging happily in the corridor.

CHAPTER TWENTY-TWO

A WRONG TURN

Boney, Squeak, Itchy, and Sam crept along the corridor, careful not to draw attention to themselves. Itchy craned his neck, as though expecting the hugging clones to appear any second. "You told us before that we needed to turn left," he said to Sam.

Sam pushed her hair behind her ears. "I know. But we don't really have a choice now. I'm hoping this passageway connects up with the one we were on—or that we'll find another way out altogether."

"Haven't these aliens ever heard of signs?" Itchy grumbled. "How do they find their way around this white jungle?"

"There's another passageway around the corner," Squeak said, indicating an identical-looking corridor to the left. "Perhaps it will lead us back the way we came."

The four friends took the new route. But they hadn't travelled more than a hundred feet when they heard the same strange whistle they'd heard in the blob's room, followed by a series of odd clicks and beeps coming from some unknown location in the corridor.

Boney searched for the source of the sound. "What *is* that?!"

"I don't know," Itchy said. "But whenever we hear that whistle, something bad happens."

Squeak looked at his feet. "The floor is starting to shake."

"It's the Itchys!" Sam cried, pointing to the end of the corridor. "Run for it!"

The red-headed clones appeared, stomping their slime-soaked sneakers robotically as they marched.

Itchy took off, Henry bouncing and squawking in his sling. "Why can't they just leave us alone?"

"You tell me!" Boney shouted. "They're your clones."

Squeak ran, his messenger bag bouncing against his back. "I'm really getting tired of this."

"There's got to be a way out of here!" Sam sprinted to the front of the group, her legs a blur.

The clones growled and moaned, the gunshot of marching feet reverberating off the walls of the ship.

"They're gaining on us!" Boney yelled.

Itchy gasped for air. "I haven't eaten all day. I have no energy left!"

Squeak pushed him from behind. "Keep running!"

The whistle sounded again and the clones began to shriek as they marched, stomping faster and faster.

"We're doomed!" Itchy wailed.

"There's some kind of button up ahead," Sam said. She ran to a point in the hall that looked the same as every other part of the ship except for a silver disc on the wall.

"How do we know what it is?" Squeak asked.

The clones surged, gaining on the friends.

"Just push it!" Itchy howled.

Sam slapped the button as hard as she could. An opening appeared in the wall. "It's a door! We can hide in here!" She yanked Boney, Itchy, and Squeak into the room, then found an identical silver button on the other side of the wall and smacked it, shutting the door against the rising hordes. The clones hit the door in a rush, banging and pounding viciously. Doubled over, hands on knees, the four friends choked and wheezed, trying to catch their breath.

"That was close," Squeak rasped.

Boney puffed. "You can say that again."

Itchy coughed. "Please don't."

"Oh!" Sam suddenly exclaimed.

Staring back at them from behind a white console were two startled blue aliens, their faces the very picture of anguish. They were tall and thin and hunched over, their bulbous heads seemingly too large for their thin bodies. They'd obviously been caught off guard, as they'd barely had the opportunity to right themselves from whatever it was they were doing before they were so rudely interrupted. One was leaning toward a microphone of sorts, a silver whistle dangling from his horrified lips. The other sat poised, a coffee mug held midway to his mouth.

"Fifth-level Blues," Sam whispered in awe.

The four friends shifted uncomfortably on their feet. The aliens seemed equally uncomfortable, staring awkwardly back, until the one with the mug gave a half-hearted wave. Boney, Squeak, Itchy, and Sam waved limply back, the Itchy clones pounding relentlessly on the door behind them. The alien with the mug continued to stare as he slowly leaned into the microphone and gave a series of hesitant clicks and beeps. This caused the pounding in the hall to mysteriously stop. It was immediately replaced with muffled shuffling and meeping outside the door. No one said anything for the longest time until Boney stepped forward.

"Um . . . are you in charge here?"

The aliens looked nervously at each other and turned to look at Boney, shrugging and blinking their eyes.

Squeak leaned toward Boney. "They may not speak English."

Boney cleared his throat, then spoke, slow and loud, exaggerating every word. "Are . . . you . . . in . . . charge . . . here?"

He waited for the aliens to answer, but they just kept bobbing their heads back and forth and looking at each other and flopping their hands around. After a long stretch of this, Itchy grew frustrated and stepped up beside Boney.

"Well? Are you in charge here?" he demanded. "Because we want some answers!" He flung his hand toward the aliens, sending a glob of green slime arcing across the room and splattering in a large starburst on the pristine white console.

The aliens shrunk back in disgust, blinking and bobbing until the one with the mug eventually placed his cup on the console and picked up a clunky headset. He wrestled to put it on and began talking, a stream of Punjabi and then Spanish gibberish blaring over the loudspeakers. The four friends covered their ears as the alien twisted a dial on the device and smacked it several times.

"Well," he finally gurgled in the Queen's English, "I suppose we're it, yes."

"So you DO understand us," Itchy said.

The alien shrugged and nodded. The one with the whistle put a headset on, too.

"We can communicate in over a thousand forms of language," he gurgled.

"A thousand and one if you include Simultus," the one with the mug corrected him.

"Right, of course," the first one agreed. "I always forget to include that one. It's really just a dialect."

"Right."

"So . . . you run this ship?" Boney interjected.

The aliens looked at each other, covered the microphones on their headsets with their hands, and began arguing furiously in their own language.

After much arm waving and several exchanged shoves, the one with the whistle spoke into his mic. "Yes, I suppose you could say that."

"Why did you clone me?" Itchy jumped in. "Do you think you can just go around cloning people and get away with it?"

The aliens slouched with shame.

"We're actually quite sorry about that," the one with the mug said. "We didn't mean for things to get so . . . out of control."

"You never should have seen the clones," the one with the whistle explained. "It was meant to be an 'up and down' sort of operation."

The alien with the mug gave a high-pitched laugh. "'Up and down'? You mean 'in and out.' Adjust your translator!"

The alien fumbled with the dial on his headset. "Errr . . . uh . . . yes . . . okay . . . there we go. It was just meant to be a quick job."

Itchy scowled. "Well, your 'quick job' has caused me a lot of trouble. There are copies of me every-where — I'm wanted by the police — not to mention the fact that you almost killed us in the room with that . . . *blob*."

The aliens nodded sympathetically.

"It's so hard to find good help these days," the one with the whistle said.

"Yes, quite difficult," the other agreed.

"But not to worry," the first one continued. "We would have disposed of the clones when we were finished."

"Yes," the other said. "You would never have known we were even here." He waved his hand through the air to show how painless the whole operation was sup-posed to have been.

"Then why did you clone me and Squeak?" Boney asked.

The aliens froze. The one with the mug spoke. "That was just a fail-safe, in case the redheads didn't work out."

The alien with the whistle tapped on his temple. "And they almost didn't. They're not very bright."

"Hey!" Itchy protested. "I'm standing right here."

"Oh yes, of course. Sorry."

"What exactly were you trying to achieve with all of this?" Squeak asked.

The aliens drummed their fingers together.

"Nothing too universe-shattering," the one with the mug said.

"We just needed a little fill-up," the other explained. "We were almost finished when you arrived . . . unfortunately."

The alien with the mug shot his colleague a worried look. "Not that we're unhappy to see you," he said. "It's just . . . we've hit a bit of a snag."

"If by 'snag' you mean . . . your blob blowing up . . . I can explain that," Boney said.

The aliens waved their hands politely. "Oh no, no, no. No need to apologize."

"But . . . we never expected you to show up armed," the alien with the whistle said.

"Armed?" Sam questioned, joining the conversation.

The alien pointed to Henry and the kittens.

Sam looked puzzled. "You're kidding, right?"

The aliens shook their heads.

Sam walked toward the console. "But these are help-less little creatures. They wouldn't hurt anyone." She held Fluffy up for the aliens to see.

"Please, no!" the aliens cried, recoiling in fright and hiding behind one another. "Don't make us look at it. *Please!* We'll tell you anything you want to know!"

"Yes, *anything!*"

"But he's a harmless little kitten," Sam cooed, taking another step closer.

"We needed some gas!" the alien with the whistle blurted out, then cowered behind his hands.

"Gas?"

"I don't get it," Itchy said.

"To run the ship?" Squeak suggested.

"Yes, yes!" the aliens confirmed, pointing at Squeak. "The weird kid with the stupid goggles gets it."

Squeak blinked indignantly. "My goggles aren't stupid . . ."

Sam placed Fluffy back in his sling. "You mean . . . all of this was for gas?"

The aliens nodded like bobble-heads.

"So . . . you're not trying to create a human-alien hybrid?" she asked.

The aliens gave her a questioning look.

"Whatever for?" the first one said.

Squeak and Sam looked at each other and shrugged. Boney pulled on his long chin. "This has been a very odd day."

Itchy sighed impatiently. "Would someone please tell me what's going on?"

CHAPTER TWENTY-THREE

THE ALIENS EXPLAIN

Squeak stepped toward the console. He squinted behind his goggles at the aliens. "So . . . let me get this straight . . . that blob—"

"—Our Flatulous," the alien with the mug corrected him.

"VERY expensive creature," the other alien said. "Cost a fortune, not to mention the dozens of workers we've hired to wrangle it over the years."

"Yes, but grey men are cheap," the first alien said.

"A dime a dozen," the other agreed.

Boney's face fell. "But we killed your blob by feeding it clones."

"It was old," the first alien said, dismissing Boney's concern.

"REALLY old," the second one said. "We would have had to acquire a new one soon anyway. Clones never agreed with it. Too much protein. You couldn't possibly have known that."

Squeak coughed to get their attention. "So . . . your *Flatulous* required sugar to create noxious gases through the digestive process . . . which you then harvested as fuel—"

The whistle alien raised his finger. "And pressurized using a three-stage diaphragm compressor . . ."

Squeak nodded. "Taking into account the compression efficiency as a ratio of theoretical temperature rise and heat loss versus the actual numbers."

"Exactly," the aliens said.

Itchy turned to Boney. "Do you have any idea what they're talking about?"

"Wait a minute," Sam said, obviously distressed. "Why would you use such an antiquated method to propel your ship? There are far less dangerous and more environmentally conscientious ways to travel through space that don't have such a negative impact on delicate ecosystems."

Her question hung in the air as the aliens exchanged worried looks once again.

"Well . . ." the first one began but was interrupted by the second, who threw his hands in the air.

"For the love of Zoilus, we dropped out!"

"Mobius, please!" the other alien said.

"What's the point of trying to hide it, Servil?"

"Dropped out of what?" Sam asked.

"School," Mobius confessed.

Servil pouted. "It was too difficult. All those rules and equations and the ENDLESS homework."

"So here we are," Mobius said. "Stuck on some silly little planet in a galaxy far, far away."

"The earth isn't silly," Itchy snipped.

Servil elbowed Mobius in the ribs. "You're doing it again . . ."

"Oh, right. I always forget how sensitive humans are. It's a lovely little place. We just don't know how to get out of here. As we said earlier, the only reason we came at all was to fill up our gas tank. We had no idea we'd end up shipwrecked."

Servil massaged his eyes with his fingertips. "What an infernal mess."

Sam considered the problem for a moment. "Why don't you just reroute your impulsion system?"

"Sure, sure," Servil agreed. "Except—*we don't know how.*"

"We skipped that day in school," Mobius said.

Itchy stepped forward. "So . . . if you're such *losers,* how did you get this ship and all these little grey guys to work for you?"

Mobius pointed a skinny blue finger at Servil. "His father is quite influential back on Zoilus. He gave us this old clunker just to get rid of us."

"Mobius!" Servil admonished.

"It's true and you know it," Mobius insisted.

Servil hung his head. "He's right. My father can't stand the sight of me. He'd rather throw money around just to get me out of his hair."

"Your father has hair?" Itchy asked.

Servil waved his hand in the air. "It's just a figure of speech."

"Servil is an embarrassment to his family," Mobius added.

"It can't be that bad," Sam said.

"Oh, it is," Mobius assured her.

Servil nodded sadly. "My father's going to be angry when he discovers we ditched the ship and lost Our Flatulous."

"Well, what does he expect?" Mobius bristled. "He should have given us something nicer than this heap of junk. We're the laughingstock of the entire universe." He kicked feebly at the side of the ship.

Sam looked at Squeak, who raised his eyebrows and nodded.

"We can show you how to reroute your impulsion

system," she offered. "That way you won't get into trouble — and you'll never have to use dirty fuel ever again."

Servil jumped up from his chair. "Could you?"

"Just direct us to your engine room," Squeak said. "If you have the parts we need, it shouldn't be too difficult to set it up."

"Oh hurrah!" Mobius cheered. He clapped his hands, then grabbed Servil and began dancing him around behind the console.

"Of course . . . we only understand how these propulsion techniques work in theory," Squeak confessed. "We've never really done them before."

Sam turned to Squeak. "It's not as if we're at risk of blowing them up or anything."

"No," Squeak agreed. "There's no fear of that. The worst that could happen is a total system failure."

"Would we go down with the ship?" Mobius asked.

"No," Squeak said. "You may just be stranded here for life."

The alien shrugged. "I'm willing to take that chance. Then we won't have to rely on slimy blobs to fuel our ship." He wrenched Servil by the arm and spun him around and around until the alien's pale blue skin took on a sickly tinge of green.

Itchy interrupted the celebration. "Just a minute.

We're not going anywhere to do anything until I've had something to eat. I'm starving."

"Of course, you have to eat," Mobius said sympathetically. He reached under the console and produced a white box, handing it to Itchy. It was filled with chocolate-glazed doughnuts. "We took them from one of your clones," he explained. "The chocolate ones are our favourite."

Itchy eyed the doughnuts, sniffed one, and began shovelling them in, one after the other, swallowing in big gulps. The aliens watched with fascination as Itchy finished the entire box and licked his fingers before letting out a big, satisfied burp. Boney leaned toward Squeak. "Maybe we could just leave Itchy in place of the Flatulous."

"I heard that!" Itchy said, as Mobius reached under the console and produced another box of doughnuts.

CHAPTER TWENTY-FOUR

THE ENGINE ROOM

Mobius raised a little silver remote and pushed a button, opening the door. The hordes of Itchys were still bumping and meeping like confused zombies in the corridor. Henry squawked the second he saw the clones. The kittens hissed and growled.

Mobius cussed, and a long series of bleeps blared from the translator. "Servil . . . could you make a call for a clean-up in corridor four?"

Servil leaned into the microphone and pressed a switch. He began talking in a series of clicks and blips. Within seconds, a dozen grey aliens in blue overalls scuttled up and began herding the clones like cattle down the hall.

"What's going to happen to them?" Itchy asked between doughnut bites.

"We'll just send them back where they came from," Mobius said.

"What do you mean?"

Servil made a pressing motion in the air with his finger. "There's a delete key on the clone machine. All you have to do is press it."

Itchy's eyes grew wide with horror.

"It's all very painless," Mobius assured him.

"Completely painless," Servil said.

Itchy licked the chocolate from his lips. "But . . . where do they go?"

Mobius gave a quick whistle. "Back into the machine. Clones are completely recyclable."

"Hmmm. Good to know." Itchy pulled another doughnut from the box.

Once the clones were sent on their way, Mobius ushered the four friends into the hall. "Shall we?"

Boney, Itchy, Squeak, and Sam followed the two aliens through the stark white corridors of the spaceship to the engine room. They seemed to have been walking around and around the same hallway when Mobius finally stopped and held up the remote. He pointed to a spot on the wall and pushed the button. The door whizzed open to reveal a dirty, steam-filled room, machines pumping and banging, little grey men scurrying here and there, their faces smeared with grease, their noses pinched with clothes pegs against the smell. They looked up in surprise when they saw the humans gazing with curiosity into the room. Mobius stepped aside and gestured for the friends to enter.

"The heart of the ship," he said, with a hint of sarcasm. He handed out clothes pegs to the four friends, gave one to Servil, and kept one for himself. "It's the best we can do on our budget."

Clipping the clothes pegs on their noses, Boney, Squeak, Itchy, and Sam began to explore the room. There were valves opening and closing from giant canisters of green gas. Long glass pipes criss-crossed the room, carrying gas from the canisters to huge compressor chambers where the fuel was condensed. Several bellows heaved in and out, creating a strange rasping sound, like a dinosaur with asthma.

"It's amazing any of this works, it's so old," Squeak said.

There was a loud pop as one of the machines blew a valve, sending hot steam hissing into the air. The little men scurried faster, desperate to fix the valve and cap the steam before it filled the entire room.

Mobius sighed with exasperation. "See what we have to work with?"

"Do you think you can help us?" Servil asked.

Squeak pushed on the bridge of his goggles. "These machines are quite worn . . . but I think we should be able to find what we need. We're going to have to cannibalize parts from your existing operation." He turned to Sam for her opinion.

She stood, wrinkling her nose against the smell. "I think we should be okay."

Squeak and Sam continued to inspect the machines, pointing and nodding and making notes while Boney and Itchy loitered on the periphery, watching the little grey men scuttle and scurry about. After several minutes, Squeak and Sam returned with a list of parts they would need.

"It won't take long," Squeak said. "You've got all the right technology here, and your ship can easily be retrofitted to support the newer system. All we need is a carbon-dioxide laser, a parabolic mirror, and an absorption chamber. Your ship is already made of silicon carbide so we're ahead of the game there."

"What a relief," Servil said.

"We'll use a superconducting magnet in conjunction with the magnetic meridians of the earth to help propel the craft into the air," Sam added. "The only drawback to this system is the potential non-lethal genetic modification of plant material on the ground as well as telltale patterns at the point of takeoff and landing."

"Crop circles!" Mobius shrieked, clapping his thin blue hand to his face. "I've always wanted to lay a patch like that. When can we get started?"

Squeak handed him his list of parts. "Right away."

"Well, what are we waiting for?" Mobius chimed.

The two aliens inspected the list, then called several little grey men over. They spoke in clicks and beeps, writing a column of strange symbols down one side of Squeak's notebook and handing it to the workers. There was a flurry of activity, with Squeak and Sam giving orders and Mobius and Servil translating. Boney helped gather the necessary parts while Itchy languished on a small, mushroom-shaped seat, snacking on chocolate-glazed doughnuts and repeating Squeak's orders as though he was the one in charge.

When the work was finished, Sam, Boney, and Squeak sat back, wiping the sweat from their faces.

"Is it ready?" Mobius asked.

Sam handed him several pages torn from her note-book. "Yes. I've made notes in case you have any problems or need to make repairs. It's pretty straightforward."

"Good thinking." Mobius handed the pages to Servil.

"We also wired your remote so you can start the craft from anywhere on the ship," Squeak said. He gave Mobius the remote. "But we should perform a test run to be sure everything is in order."

Itchy stepped forward. "Before we do that, I need to ask about the clones again."

The aliens gaped at him.

"I'd like to see what happens to them."

"Sure," Mobius said. "We don't mind, do we, Servil?"

"No, not at all," Servil pleasantly agreed.

Mobius walked over to a monitor on the wall and touched the screen. Multiple images of the ship appeared, and he shuffled through them until he found the one he was looking for. He enlarged the image so that it filled the entire screen. "There they are," he said, pointing to a room filled with Itchys, Boneys, and Squeaks.

"And there they go," Servil said, pressing a code into the keypad on the side of the screen.

A blue light flashed. The room where hundreds of clones once stood was now empty.

Itchy stared at the screen. "They're gone."

Mobius snapped his fingers. "Just like that."

"What about the clone the police put in jail?" Itchy asked.

Mobius smiled. "History."

"What about the warehouse in the woods?" Squeak said. "Where did it go?"

Mobius snapped his fingers again. "Folded like a circus tent."

"An entire building?"

"It was really more of an illusion than a building," Servil explained. "Think of it as . . . an extraterrestrial sleight of hand."

"And the DNA for creating the clones?" Sam asked. "Is it still in your data bank?"

Mobius called up a folder on the screen and hit delete. "Done."

The four friends exchanged looks.

"You don't have anything to worry about," Servil said. "Clones are only good on the planet they originate from. They're no use to us anywhere else." He turned to Sam. "By the way, that Disruptor device is a little piece of genius. We could have really used it around here."

Sam beamed. "Thank you. Except that it only works the first couple times you deploy the rays. Subsequent use seems to have less effect on the clones."

"Maybe you just need to reconfigure the signal so that it's slightly different each time," Squeak suggested. "That way the clones can't assimilate the frequency — "

"Yeah, anyway, we thought it was brilliant," Mobius interjected. "Where did you get the idea?"

Sam pulled a small beige hardcover book from her bag and held it up. "I used the basic premise in this dissertation and simply modified the application. I met the author at a trade show."

Mobius read the title and let out a grunt. "*Satellite Technology!* Ugh! That was one of our textbooks back on Zoilus."

Boney narrowed his eyes. "How could it be one of your textbooks on Zoilus?"

"Yes, how could it be?" Sam asked. "I met the author."

Servil coughed nervously. Mobius flopped his hands around. "I must be confusing it with something else." He gave an apprehensive laugh.

Sam put her hands on her hips. "Unless you're implying that the author is an alien . . . ?"

The Odds eyed each other. Squeak raised his notebook and pencil. "If you don't mind, we have a number of questions we'd like to ask."

Mobius's eyes twitched. "Of course . . . ask whatever you want . . ."

He looked at Servil, who forced a smile, then shot out his hand, hitting a button on the wall.

A hatch fell open in the floor and the troop of friends and their animal companions were sucked from the room in a blast of cold air. They dropped, yelling and hollering and squawking and mewing through a long tube to be spit out with a heavy thud onto the ground. There was a blinding flash, and the spaceship launched into the sky, punching through the clouds. Itchy and Boney and Squeak and Sam coughed and gasped for air, struggling to breathe in the heavier atmosphere outside the spaceship. Henry clucked and the kittens mewed.

"How rude!" Sam blurted out the minute she caught her breath.

Boney spit dirt from his mouth. "After everything we did for them."

"At least we know the light propulsion system works," Squeak said, rubbing his shoulder.

Itchy lay splayed across the ground like a discarded plate of spaghetti. He groaned feebly. "I'm hungry."

Boney stood up and helped Itchy to his feet. Sam and Squeak bumped heads as they tried to stand, blushing instantly. The four friends brushed the leaves and dirt from their clothes, then adjusted their slings, making sure the kittens and Henry were all right.

"I'm hungry," Itchy said again, scratching Henry on the neck.

Squeak consulted his watch. "I'm not surprised. It's nearly four o'clock."

Boney gazed at the ragged hole left in the clouds by the spaceship. The sunlight shone through its tattered edges, dancing through the leaves as it reached for the forest floor. He breathed in deeply. "Come on, guys. Let's go home."

CHAPTER TWENTY-FIVE

A NEW ORDER

Boney, Itchy, Squeak, and Sam sat around the table at the clubhouse, happily eating saltine crackers with peanut butter and honey and slurping on cans of ginger ale. Sam used the overturned mop bucket as a seat because there were only three chairs. Toques and combat boots littered the clubhouse floor. Henry and the kittens were enjoying their own snack, eating from bowls of chow.

"Where'd you learn to fight like that?" Boney asked Sam. "You were really doing a number on those clones."

"Please don't say 'clones,'" Itchy sputtered through a mouthful of crackers.

Sam leaned back against the wall. "My dad's a black belt. I've been studying with him since I was a child."

"Your dad sounds so cool," Squeak said. "I really want to meet him."

Sam thought about this for a second. "I think you'd like him. He's actually rather . . . odd . . . by most people's standards."

The boys nodded with approval over their cans of pop.

"Well, I for one am happy you have such mad skills," Boney confessed.

"Me too," Squeak said.

"Me three," Itchy agreed.

The four friends munched quietly for a while, processing the events of the day.

"Do you think there really are aliens living among us?" Sam finally broke the silence. She pulled the *Satellite Technology* book from her bag.

Squeak studied the pale beige cover. "It's highly probable. Statistically speaking, it's more likely that aliens are living among us than not."

"We could contact the author of the book," Boney suggested.

Itchy shook his head. "No way. I've had enough of aliens for the rest of my life."

"It was pretty exciting to see the ship from the inside," Sam said. "I think I'm going to write a paper for *Space Exploration* magazine. I thought you might like to help me." She looked at Squeak.

Squeak giggled involuntarily, covering his mouth with his hand as he blushed. Itchy rolled his eyes. Sam continued.

"And I have another proposition—for all of you."

The Odds waited expectantly.

"I'd like to propose a joint project for the NASA Revolutionary Vehicles and Concepts Competition. I'd like you to help me reproduce the light technology we created for Mobius and Servil."

Itchy moaned. "Don't say their names. We don't want to encourage them to come back."

"I doubt they'll be back anytime soon," Boney said.

Squeak beamed at Sam, trying not to smile too brightly. "That's really kind of you to include us in the competition. I'd be delighted to help."

"Me too," Boney said. "That's really generous of you."

All three turned to Itchy. He shifted uncomfortably in his chair.

"I guess it'd be okay," he finally conceded.

"Great!" Sam cheered. "It's going to be really exciting!"

Squeak stood up at the table and cleared his throat. "I'd like to forward my own proposal. After careful consideration of the events over the last week, I'd like to recommend Sam as a candidate for the Order of Odd Fellows."

Sam glowed. "Really?" She looked around at the boys' faces.

Boney nodded enthusiastically. "I'd like to second that motion."

Itchy sprawled in his chair, scratching like a distracted monkey at his bramble-bush hair. "I have a problem with that."

The smile slipped from Sam's face.

Itchy sat up and stared soberly at his friends. "Sam can't be an Odd Fellow."

"Why not?" Squeak demanded. "She's just as good as any of us here—better even!"

"That's right," Boney jumped in. "What issue could you possibly have with allowing Sam to be a member of our club?"

Itchy waved in Sam's direction. "Look at her. Anyone can see she's not an Odd *Fellow*." He stood up importantly, placing both hands on top of the table. "I propose we form a new organization. I propose we establish the *Odd Squad*."

"The Odd Squad!" Boney and Squeak exclaimed, staring at each other in surprise.

"I like it," Boney said.

"Me too," Squeak agreed.

Itchy grinned, obviously proud of himself. "It's all-inclusive."

Squeak raised a finger. "I think the correct term is 'gender-neutral.'"

"Sure, whatever." Itchy hitched up his pants. "And there's one more thing . . . We're going to need a new method of late-night communication. I don't think there's a tube long enough to reach Sam's house from here."

All eyes turned to Squeak.

Squeak raised an eyebrow. "I have some things in mind. But nothing I care to divulge at this time."

"Good enough!" Itchy decreed, pounding his skinny fist on the table. He lifted his ginger ale to his lips and emptied the contents in one giant, noisy swig before releasing a gigantic burp.

Boney and Squeak looked in horror at Sam.

Sam stood, held her ginger ale in the air, and proceeded to guzzle the entire drink even faster than Itchy. When the can was empty, she crumpled it with one hand and ripped the biggest, juiciest, wall-shaking burp the Odds had ever heard. The boys roared with appreciation. Boney clapped Sam on the back. Itchy gawked in admiration.

"How'd you do that?" he asked.

Sam tapped her sternum. "It's all in the diaphragm."

The four friends burst out laughing.

Itchy walked to the side of the clubhouse and tore the NO GIRLS ALLOWED sign from the wall. "We won't be needing this anymore." He made a big show of trying to break the sign over his knee. After several failed attempts, he gave up and simply tossed the sign out of one of the clubhouse windows, wiping his hands together with satisfaction. "And one more thing . . ." He pointed to the mop bucket Sam was using as a seat. "We're going to need another chair."

"Done!" Boney said.

Itchy walked to the cooler and rustled a couple more cans of ginger ale from the ice, tossing one to Sam. She caught it in one hand and cracked it open; the pop fizzed with an effervescent hiss.

"To the Odd Squad!" Itchy boomed, raising his ginger ale.

"To the Odd Squad!" The friends toasted, clinking their cans of pop together in the air.

Henry and the kittens looked up with curiosity from their bowls. Squeak looked at his watch and pointed at Boney.

"Your aunt's going to call you in three . . . two . . . one . . ."

"Boneeey!"

THE END